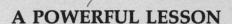

A POWERFUL LESSON

Hetty turned to the blackboard and wrote, in large letters, "G-U-S P-I-K-E."

"What's that?" Gus inquired about the incomprehensible squiggles.

"It's your name."

Gus's eyes popped as wide as if Hetty King had pulled a jackrabbit out of her ear.

"My name! No guff . . . that's my name?"

"It is," Hetty assured him, quelling the amusement of the rest of the room with a severe glance. "And you can start to learn to print it by copying these letters over and over again on the slate. Here's your chalk. And don't stop until I say so."

Gus took the slate and chalk from Hetty.

In Gus's mind, his new teacher had just assumed the stature of a minor divinity. If Hetty King could write his name out for him, just like that, why, she must know about everything else there is to know. And if she knew all that, how could she do any wrong?

Also available in the Road to Avonlea series from Bantam Skylark books

Aunt Hetty's Ordeal

Storybook written by

Gail Hamilton

Based on the Sullivan Films Production
written by Marlene Matthews
adapted from the novels of

Lucy Maud Montgomery

A BANTAM SKYLARK BOOK®
NEW YORK • TORONTO • LONDON • SYDNEY • AUCKLAND

Based on the Sullivan Films Production produced by Sullivan Films Inc. in association with CBC and the Disney Channel with the participation of Telefilm Canada adapted from Lucy Maud Montgomery's novels.

Teleplay written by Marlene Matthews.
Copyright © 1991 by Sullivan Films Distribution, Inc.

This edition contains the complete text
of the original hardcover edition.
NOT ONE WORD HAS BEEN OMITTED.

RL 6, 008–012

AUNT HETTY'S ORDEAL

A Bantam Skylark Book / published by arrangement with
HarperCollins Publishers Ltd.

PUBLISHING HISTORY
HarperCollins edition published 1992
Bantam edition / April 1993

ISBN 0-553-48039-1

Bantam Books are published by Bantam Books, a division of Bantam
Doubleday Dell Publishing Group, Inc. Its trademark, consisting of the
words "Bantam Books" and the portrayal of a rooster, is Registered in
U.S. Patent and Trademark Office and in other countries. Marca
Registrada. Bantam Books, 666 Fifth Avenue, New York, New York
10103.

PRINTED IN THE UNITED STATES OF AMERICA
OPM   0   9   8   7   6   5   4   3   2   1

Chapter One

Breathes there a man with a soul so dead,
Who never to himself hath said,
'This is my home, my native land,'
Whose heart has ne'er within him burned...
...to his home, his footsteps...um...footsteps...

Sara Stanley stumbled over the last line, then trailed to an exasperated halt. It was hard enough trying to learn poetry while painting a fence, but to be afflicted with such a poem! She dabbled her brush in the paint can in dissatisfaction, almost spattering Aunt Hetty in the process. Hetty was also hard at work outside Rose Cottage while she listened to Sara practice.

"Oh, Aunt Hetty," Sara burst out, "it's such a dull poem. We'll bore them to death!"

This wasn't exactly the sort of thing one said to Miss Hetty King, Avonlea's schoolteacher. Hetty had picked out that poem very carefully for her pupils to memorize and didn't like having her choice protested by a twelve-year-old critic with paint smears on her nose.

"I'll be the judge of what's boring, Sara Stanley," Hetty answered tartly, giving one of the fence pickets a smart slap with her brush.

Hetty King was the sort of woman who, once she'd made up her mind about a thing, considered the matter closed. Every angular line of her, from her hair vigorously subdued into a bun to the snap with which she handled a paintbrush, proclaimed the fact that her principles didn't bend and her opinions didn't change. And the more one argued with her, the more set in her ways she was likely to become.

Sara rolled her eyes skyward. Though her Aunt Hetty had many admirable qualities, imagination was certainly not one of them. Sara, on the other hand, was so brimful of imagination that Aunt Hetty was beyond guessing what the girl might be up to next. Naturally, Sara considered herself more than qualified to tell what brand of verse would spellbind a crowd.

"Aunt Hetty, it's the Lieutenant Governor's reception. The poem should be more inspiring."

The Lieutenant Governor was, after all, the representative of the Crown in Prince Edward Island. The reception, to be held at the White Sands Hotel, was the most exciting thing to happen around Avonlea for months, maybe even years, so choosing just the right poem for the school to recite was vital. Something hopelessly romantic was what Sara had in mind, with a fair maiden wasting away, ignored by a cruel lover, or a thrilling storm at sea, after which the drowned sailors come back as ghosts to moan wrenching last farewells. Oh, a tale so deliciously, heartrendingly pathetic that even the dignified Lieutenant Governor would end up with a heaving bosom and tears glinting in his eyes.

In Montreal, where she used to live, Sara had been to many elegant receptions with her father, and she knew the effect Hetty's dreary, patriotic poem would have on people out for a gala evening, expecting to enjoy themselves.

She also feared the effect on her Aunt Hetty should the poem prove the disaster Sara privately predicted. Hetty King considered herself a leader of the community, and took her position very seriously. In fact, in the opinion of a number of Avonlea busybodies, she took it far too seriously. So, if her school presented a poem that put even the

Lieutenant Governor to sleep, it might be a very long time before gleefully wagging tongues let Hetty King live the humiliation down.

Luckily, before anyone could get into an argument about the nature of inspiration, Sara's Aunt Olivia straightened up at the far end of the yard, where she had been painting the corner post. Olivia had spotted the mailman rattling down the road towards them on his old red bicycle. What's more, he had a handful of letters for Rose Cottage clutched in one hand. Since the arrival of mail was always an event, Olivia trotted out and took the letters so neatly that the mailman barely had to touch the ground with his foot. With a nod and a wave, he peddled on around the corner, bouncing over potholes as he went. Olivia turned back to the house with her booty.

As she turned, leafing through the letters in her hand, she came to a large white envelope and stopped in her tracks. The next minute, she was racing over the grass towards the others, waving her find.

"Hetty! Look! It's an official letter from the Queens County Board of Education! Hetty, nobody gets an official letter, unless..." Olivia's eyes danced with a sudden, dazzling possibility, "unless it's a promotion! That's it. It's a promotion to superintendent!"

Hetty stopped painting instantly, barely managing not to drop her brush. As befitted the head of the King clan, she made an attempt to hang onto her dignity and not look so wildly excited as Olivia.

"Perhaps it's a promotion of sorts," she murmured, with as much modesty as she could muster on such short notice. "Oh, I will admit the timing would be right, with the Lieutenant Governor's reception and all..."

On this occasion, even Hetty found some imagination. As she took the letter from Olivia, she let out a tremulous breath, lost in a vision of herself gliding about at the grand social event as the newly promoted school superintendent. She'd be one of the honored guests. Why, even the Lieutenant Governor himself would have to single her out.

As she tore open the envelope, a flush of excitement climbed Hetty's cheek. A promotion had been in the back of her mind for a very long time now, though she would rather have been hung by her thumbs than admit it out loud. She had put in more than enough service in Avonlea to earn the recognition. Besides, she just itched to get her hands on the rest of the county schools, to show them a thing or two about how education should be run.

Next to her, Sara and Olivia exchanged happy, expectant glances, never doubting that Hetty was at last going to get something her heart had been set on, and which she richly deserved. So when Hetty finally got the letter out of the envelope and smoothed it out against the breeze, they were much surprised to see the flush on her cheek suddenly mottle into a dark and angry red.

" 'Dear Hetty,' " she read aloud. " 'Just a note to let you know I've been promoted. I'm now Provincial Superintendent of Schools. I'm starting a province-wide tour and plan a special stop in Avonlea. I do so look forward to seeing everyone, and especially having a look at the old school. Yours truly, Muriel Stacey.' "

By the time she'd sputtered to the end of this bombshell, Hetty's lips were aquiver and her face was burning; she was unable, for the moment, even to comment on the letter's contents. Olivia, who had started all the furor with her extravagant speculations, was equally crestfallen.

"Oh, Hetty..."

"Who's Muriel Stacey?" Sara asked. Sara might have been hazy about niceties of rank in the Board of Education, but she knew that, to have this much effect on Hetty, the mysterious Muriel Stacey must be a wonder.

Olivia shot Sara a warning look. "Oh, she went to teachers' college with Aunt Hetty, and they both taught in Avonlea, but it was years ago."

"Muriel Stacey!" Hetty exploded indignantly, crumpling the letter into a tight little ball. Her eyes blazed, speaking volumes about those far-off days of teaching together. Sweet, selfless companionship had not, perhaps, been Hetty's stock-in-trade in those days.

"It's nice...that she's coming for a visit, Hetty," Olivia put in hastily. In contrast to her older sister's peppery personality, Olivia was a peacemaker, always looking on the bright side of things and trying her best to smooth uncomfortable upsets—a fortunate trait in anyone having to share living quarters with Hetty King. Sara and Olivia had often been confederates in their struggles against Hetty's somewhat exalted ideas of her own authority at Rose Cottage.

Hetty let out a great harumph. "Don't be ridiculous, Olivia. She's not coming to visit. She's coming to inspect my school."

Hetty ran the Avonlea school to suit herself, and did a smart job of it, too. She had enough trouble tolerating the regular school inspectors, never mind old companions who had just been rudely promoted over her head.

"But Aunt Hetty, that's not what she said in her letter," Sara put in ingenuously. Sara was still young enough to believe that written words meant exactly what they said.

"She's far too weasely to say it," Hetty hissed, turning a gimlet eye on her niece. "But it is there, between the lines, plain as day. Well, I don't need inspecting. And neither does my school!"

"Will Miss Stacey go to the Lieutenant Governor's reception?"

Sometimes, Sara just didn't know when to stop. She had asked the question that was first in her mind, not warned in the least by Olivia's swift grimace.

The spots on Aunt Hetty's cheeks grew even redder. "Oh, she wouldn't miss it for all the tea in China. Ah yes, that's why she's rushing up here—to hog the limelight!"

Oh, no! Both Sara and Olivia regarded Hetty with suddenly dismayed glances, for Hetty was getting a notion into her head. And once Hetty got a notion into her head, it usually took an earthquake to shake it out again. In the meantime, with Hetty believing that Muriel Stacey had somehow done her wrong, life would grow impossible around Rose Cottage. And, from the look of it, most of the fun would be taken out of the much-anticipated Lieutenant Governor's reception.

Indeed, for all her excellent traits, Hetty King, at that moment, did not present the image of a graceful and generous loser. She was already swelling up with outrage, speaking as though Muriel Stacey had deliberately stolen something that rightfully belonged in Hetty's pocket. Her nostrils twitched. The poor, innocent letter was crushed even further in Hetty's fist and crammed into the pocket of her work smock. Catching the long faces of her two companions, she gave her chin a jerk.

"What are you two staring at? There's work to be done! Let's do it! Paint!"

Sara and Olivia exchanged another glance and, with none of their former enthusiasm, went back to work. But when Hetty stuffed the letter in her pocket and picked up her brush, she attacked the fence with so much force that the posts shook and white paint flew through the pickets to spatter the grass on the other side.

Sara and Olivia jumped out of range in alarm, and Olivia flung a protective arm around her niece. Wishing she'd never seen the postman, Olivia began to suspect that there might be a rougher time ahead than either she or Sara supposed.

Chapter Two

If the prospect of the Lieutenant Governor's reception was causing anxiety at Rose Cottage, it was generating a positive uproar at the Avonlea general store. The reason for this pandemonium was the arrival of all the new hats ordered by the ladies of Avonlea for the occasion. The women had spotted the freight wagon rumbling into the village and had descended on Lawson's general store before Mrs. Lawson could manage to lift the hat boxes from the crate.

In front of the long wooden counter, Mrs. Inglis, Mrs. Spencer, Mrs. Potts and Mrs. Biggins scrambled to snatch their prizes from under the tissue paper and jam them on their heads. Completely disregarding Mrs. Lawson's attempts to keep order, they jostled each other for a look in the tall old mirror kept in a corner for just such a purpose. And, as usual, the women were not pleased with what they saw.

"Mrs. Lawson, I remember plain as day, I ordered feathers!" cried Mrs. Biggins, cocking her head under a mass of blindingly white artificial flowers. The flowers were incongruously interspersed with artificial cherries that rattled when she moved. She'd have to stand like a statue at the reception, or have everyone twisting their necks around to see where the noise was coming from.

"Just let me check my list," breathed Mrs. Lawson, frazzled already. "They've never made a mistake before, but this is a big order."

"And mine had flowers," chimed in Mrs. Potts, a woman who made it her business to be dissatisfied with everything except a juicy piece of gossip. "This is all wrong!"

As Mrs. Potts jerked the squat navy straw off her head, Mrs. Inglis frowned at her own shocking-pink broad-brim, and even Mrs. Spencer, whose hat suited her admirably, started to look as if she, too, had found grounds for complaint.

Afraid she might soon have a general revolt to deal with, Mrs. Lawson raised her hands placatingly. "Now, ladies, calm down," she pleaded. "Just calm down. I'll work it out."

Mrs. Lawson searched hurriedly for the invoice and cast a reproachful glance at her husband. She would get no help at all from that quarter. Safe behind the kegs of nails at the back of the store, Mr. Lawson was keeping well out of the way. Harness and seed grain and barrels of flour he could deal with, but the choosing of ladies' hats was far too dangerous a territory for him to enter. He left all the thorny problems of ladies' apparel squarely to his wife.

As Mrs. Lawson shoved the spilled tissue paper

aside, the newly arrived stack of newspapers on the counter underneath came to light. Mrs. Spencer forgot about her hat, pounced on the Avonlea *Chronicle*, and began paging through it avidly. Just as Hetty King and Sara Stanley stepped in through the door, Mrs. Spencer found the notice she had been looking for.

"Ladies, ladies," she cried, waving her hand for quiet, "here it is. 'Miss Stacey,'" she began reading out, "'who is coming to Avonlea to inspect the school, will be staying at Biggins's Boarding House, owned by Mrs. Myrtle Biggins. Miss Stacey, who has had many articles published on her modern views of education, has won a number of awards, including the gold graduation medal at Queens College.'"

Having once entered the store, Hetty couldn't very well turn around and flee. Trapped between the village women and the broom display, Hetty was forced to listen rigidly as Mrs. Spencer gushed on about Muriel Stacey. Mrs. Potts, who had had her pretensions punctured many a time by Hetty's sharp tongue, soon noticed how badly the article was putting the teacher's nose out of joint. Seeing a chance to take a fine potshot in return, she smiled snidely and turned round.

"Wasn't that the year you came in second, Hetty?" she inquired. "Lost the medal to Muriel Stacey by three marks."

"Uh, four," corrected Mrs. Spencer sweetly, casting a sidelong glance at Hetty.

It was amazing what people could remember when they needed wounding information. Hetty stiffened so much Sara could actually hear her aunt's corset squeak.

"I think she cheated on those exams," Hetty whispered fiercely to Sara, grabbing at any straw to defend herself in this den of clacking tongues she had accidentally stepped into.

Delighted with the effect the article was having, Mrs. Spencer turned back to the newspaper and went on reading to the assembled listeners.

" '...Avonlea owes a great deal to Miss Stacey for her efforts on behalf of our children. Students such as Anne Shirley and Gilbert Blythe went on to great heights, due to her encouragement.' "

The relish in Mrs. Spencer's voice made Hetty's eyes narrow dangerously. She recovered as many shreds of her self-possession as she could and went on the offensive.

"We're all quite capable of reading the paper without your help, Sarah Spencer."

Having read enough of the article to get Hetty gratifyingly riled, Mrs. Spencer folded the paper and shot the teacher an arch look. Mrs. Potts looked even more smug.

"The truth be known," Mrs. Potts could not

resist adding, "since Muriel Stacey left, school enrollment's dropped like a stone. Why, she got children to go to school who would never have set foot in the door!"

Mrs. Potts might as well have stabbed a dagger into Hetty's bosom, for if anyone truly cared about education, it was Hetty King. Under her prickly exterior, Hetty was a deeply dedicated teacher who thought a decent education the cure for just about all the ills of the world. She drew herself up to her full height inside her dark serge dress and marched towards the counter. No one was going to accuse her of laxity when it came to the matter of enrollment.

"Far be it from me, ladies, to, uh, toot my own horn, but I have my own plans, you know, for boosting enrollment. I just don't blab about it, is all."

She glared directly at Mrs. Spencer, who only raised her eyebrows in open skepticism—a look that spurred Hetty to come up with a plan of action on the spot.

"Why, this very day, in fact, I'm off again to seek out the lost sheep of Avonlea and herd them into my fold. Oh, as I've always said, if there is an uneducated child out there, I'll find him and *drag* him into school."

From the way Hetty jutted her jaw, a whole platoon of children wouldn't have been safe from her clutches should she catch them outside the school-yard fence.

Mrs. Potts, an expert at turning the most direct words around, took swift advantage of the opening Hetty had left. "Muriel Stacey never dragged anyone," she drawled, beginning to root among the unclaimed hats to see what else she could find. "Why, children flocked to her like bees to honey."

This was a thinly veiled way of saying that Hetty King hadn't a trace of honey anywhere about her. In this, Mrs. Potts had hit a sore spot, perhaps the source of all Hetty's resentment of Muriel Stacey. Hetty, who ran her school with firm discipline and exacting order, was all too aware that children had always preferred the engaging charm of the lively Miss Stacey. Hetty's breath came hotly and she took another step forward. Things might actually have come to blows had not Mrs. Biggins jumped into the fray with her own concerns. It wasn't often the boarding house was host to such an important visitor; there were practical matters to consider.

"Hmmm. Now then, since she's staying at my place, I'll make supper the first night. Baked cod and turnips."

This seemingly simple statement brought Hetty furiously round on Mrs. Biggins. The mere proprietor of a boarding house was not going to snatch away something else due Hetty King. Miss Stacey's first meal in Avonlea was a matter of paramount social importance and would certainly set the tone for the rest of her visit.

"You'll do no such thing, Myrtle Biggins! Proper etiquette dictates I have her first. I'll not have Muriel Stacey complaining I didn't do right by her. No, no. First night, she dines at Rose Cottage, and that's that."

With that, Hetty swooped down on a flat, brown straw hat ornamented with layers of bows, which Mrs. Potts had just picked up, and snatched it clean away.

"And *that* happens to be mine, thank you. Some people have better things to do than fuss about with hats."

Her prize clutched in her fist, Hetty turned on her heel and sailed out of the store, Sara in tow. The door thumped shut after her and seemed to leave a small whirlwind in the place where Hetty had stood.

The ladies in front of the counter, for all their disdainful looks, were struck momentarily speechless. Then they all put their heads together at once to discuss the stimulating exchange. Mrs. Lawson, who liked the Kings and hated dissension of any kind, almost intervened on Hetty's behalf. However, since she was so badly outnumbered, she only shook her head and went on with her search for the bill.

Chapter Three

With Muriel Stacey's visit looming ahead and the jibes of Mrs. Potts ringing in her ears, Hetty was stirred into action. Having announced that she was bringing new pupils to school, she now had to go out and find them. A very short time after leaving the general store, Hetty was seen driving her buggy rapidly along the road, her buggy wheels throwing up sprays of gravel. She was alone and still seething about what had been said to her in the store.

"Bees to honey, indeed. Ha!"

Blackie, the horse, laid her ears back nervously at Hetty's furious mutterings. Hetty only laid another slap of the reins across the animal's rump while she gave herself up to the turmoil boiling in her breast.

"Well, Miss Muriel Know-it-all," she erupted heatedly, "I'll fill that Avonlea school full to bursting in no time. Ha!"

The old rivalry from teachers' college still rankled, alive and unforgotten even now that Hetty was quite into her middle years. And if Muriel Stacey meant to come prying into the affairs of the Avonlea school, Hetty was determined that she find not the slightest thing amiss, including the enrollment.

Extra schoolchildren, though, were hard to come by in Avonlea. Hetty had racked her brain for places to find new pupils and grown rather desperate. So desperate, in fact, that her buggy was on its way to McCorkadale's Cannery, where fish from the local fishing boats were hauled up from the holds and put into cans. The cannery had a rough, transient work force that came and went as the spirit moved. Among them, Hetty hoped she might find a few still young enough and tame enough to be hauled off to school.

The cannery was a long, rickety-looking, red-roofed building of weathered gray shingles that was conveniently located alongside its own dock. Barrels and boxes stood all around it and were stacked against the surrounding wooden sheds. Through the salt-stained windows could be seen the clanking machinery that turned out the rows of shining cans. Alarming noises issued from the interior. The doors stood open, revealing shadowy shapes moving busily about inside.

Just for an instant, Hetty hesitated. The place was apt to be full of rugged workers not at all partial to schoolteachers invading their midst. And even as she watched, those very same workers, men, women and young people, came spilling out in the lowering sun as the whistle signaled the end of the work day. Angus McCorkadale, the owner, came out among them, clipboard in hand. He was a broad, big-bellied man with jowls to his collar and a battered old hat jammed down over a bald head sprinkled round the fringes with gray. He ran his cannery with a bluff command he thought quite suited to the sort of workers he had to deal with.

"Quittin' time! Quittin' time! Quittin' time!" he boomed out, as though every weary employee, anxious to escape the noise and heat inside, did not already know the fact twice over. Angus began to stride about, issuing instructions to various sweat-stained people milling about outside the doors.

"You there," he was saying to a couple of men just as Hetty drove up abreast, "make sure those fish are on ice before you pack it in...and wash those tables down."

Any place handling fish had to be kept clean, and Angus McCorkadale did his best. Nevertheless, the ripe fragrance of fish innards billowed out across the road and choked Hetty's nostrils.

"Oooh," she gasped, recoiling, "that smell! It's...it's suffocating."

"It's an honest smell, Hetty King," Angus tossed back bluntly, wondering what on earth the woman was doing nosing about that neighborhood. "Besides, the fish belong here. You don't."

If this was a hint to leave, Hetty was not put off. She was here because she intended to do a little fishing of her own.

"I've come for a reason," she informed Angus, rapidly taking her handkerchief from her bag and pressing it to her nose. "Those boys should be in school, now that lobster season's at an end."

Angus peered over his shoulder at the objects of Hetty's scrutiny. They were a handful of large, wild-looking youths sprawled all over the dock in their fish-smeared clothes, their faces smudged with grit.

"Those hooligans?" Angus chuckled. "Ha! They'd sooner rot than get stuck in a schoolhouse."

"You think so, do you?" Hetty asserted, looking over the lads with a measuring eye. Yes, she told herself bravely, even such uncouth fellows might be civilized if only she could get them inside her classroom and into her power.

"I *know* so. Ask for yourself!"

The boys were all gaping at Hetty now and poking each other with their elbows. Ladies in starched white blouses with cameos at their throats were a rare sight in the fish cannery and therefore the occasion of much mirth.

"I—I will. Yes, I will."

Her bluff called by Angus, Hetty had no choice but to approach the boys herself. Well, Hetty had never been one to back down from a challenge, even if the challenge involved plucking would-be scholars from amongst barrels of cod on a dock. She meant to impress Muriel Stacey with her school enrollment even if she had to bring in ruffians like these to do it. Once inside the school door, no one dared stay a hooligan for long.

Climbing down from her buggy, Hetty picked up her skirts and made her way over the pitted planks of the dock to where the young people were lounging alongside the cannery.

"Boys, listen to me. I'm...I'm here to offer you a chance to get an education."

Though there were rules in Prince Edward Island about school attendance, it was often hard to enforce them. Lots of children missed out on school altogether—some from moving about the countryside, some from living too far away from a school and a great many just because they were put straight to work on the farm or the fishing boat the moment they were big enough to be of any use. Lots of folks, parents and children alike, didn't see any point in book-learning when one could get one's living by the sweat of one's back and sign anything that needed to be signed with a fine-looking "X."

The boys in front of Hetty all had that unkempt, sprawling air that meant they had run wild as wolves from infancy and had never seen the inside of a book, never mind the inside of a school. Despite their youthful ages, which ranged from about twelve upward, they were all lighting up cigarettes and pipes and regarding Hetty with an amused, superior air.

"They pay ya in school?" the biggest one asked slyly. He had hair sticking up like bits of straw in a wind from under an old, black bowler hat, and he clearly thought himself the wit of the group.

Next to him, a wiry lad with a pipe in his teeth and a pleasant, sunburnt face laughed aloud.

"It can't be less than McCorkadale is paying us now."

"Yeah, how much ya payin'?" the first fellow persisted humorously, winking sideways at his friends.

Hetty knew only too well that boys in a gang are always on the lookout for some source of fun, and she didn't mean that source to be herself. Looking about her, she spotted a low handcart used to trundle boxes of salt from shed to shed. Steadying it, Hetty stepped up on it so all could see her. A foot or two in the height department was just what she needed, she thought, to give some authority to her speech.

"Oh, look at that," cried the wiry lad, grinning. "She's doin' a play."

Hetty faced down the boys' derisive laughter and the puffs of smoke from their pipes. At her sides, her hands clenched into determined fists.

"School will change your lives. You'll see. Golden opportunities will beckon to you."

This was not exactly the sort of language to sway the minds of such shaggy young cubs as these. Ignoring Hetty, the first fellow, whose name was Pincher, turned to talk with a friend. Since Pincher was the leader, this proved a signal for the rest to go back to joking and idling too, rudely turning their backs on Hetty altogether.

All, that is, except the wiry lad with the pipe gripped between his teeth. Though he lounged as casually as the other boys, he kept his eyes intently on Hetty. He had an alert, intelligent air about him, and he seemed to possess a maverick streak of curiosity lacking in the others. He was drawn in, almost in spite of himself, and his half-lowered lids were unable to conceal the intrigued interest creeping into his eyes.

"Doors you found impenetrable will open for you," Hetty announced with ringing promise, drawing herself up as grandly as she could while balancing on an unsteady handcart encrusted with dried-up fish parts. The cart tilted sideways and Hetty's striking pose was ruined by a flapping scramble to stay upright. Pincher leered at her through one comical eye.

"She's finished the play," he crowed, making the rest of the boys, and even Angus, laugh.

By now, even Hetty saw that grandiose and abstract language was going to get her nowhere here. Conscious of Angus McCorkadale's amused gaze boring into her back, enjoying her defeat, Hetty skipped the rest of her speech and got straight to the point. No chuckling cannery owner was going to get the better of her.

"All right, how many of you want to learn to read and write, hmmm?"

This question produced such dead silence all round that Hetty might as well have asked how many present wanted to turn into toads. Yet her offer hadn't fallen upon entirely barren ground. The wiry lad took the pipe from his mouth and hitched himself forward.

"I do," he announced.

Utter astonishment rippled through his co-workers. They all twisted around to stare at the boy, who seemed almost as surprised as they at the words that had just popped out of his mouth. Hoots of derision pierced the air, and Pincher made a horrible face at the very idea of school.

Hetty, quite startled by her instant success, felt her face flush with the thrill of victory.

"Good for you, boy." She peered at her recruit more closely, then smiled in recognition. "You're Gus Pike, aren't you?"

Gus Pike had appeared in the neighborhood out of nowhere a few weeks before and had stayed for a time in Alec King's barn loft. He'd been with a trawler crew, he'd said, until the boat went down. He earned his keep by doing odd jobs for Alec, Hetty's brother, until the cannery started to hire.

The boy nodded, and Hetty turned herself around triumphantly on the handcart.

"Well, what do you say to that, Angus McCorkadale?"

Angus, though he made good use of his own reading and writing skills to run his cannery, thought education a frivolous luxury for anyone he employed. What's more, he was irritated by what he regarded as a sudden desertion by one of his hired hands. Displeased that his judgment had been proved wrong, especially in public, he glowered at Hetty in a less than sporting manner.

"I say cow chips! He's too old to learn."

Angus was sure he had a point there, because Gus had to be going on sixteen at least, practically a man and able to earn a man's wage at the cannery. Surely school was for little kids dragged there by their mothers to keep them out of mischief until they grew big enough to start earning their keep.

"Mind your language," crackled Hetty, climbing thankfully down from the cart. "You're never too old to learn."

Angus jerked his head at Gus, addressing him grumpily.

"It's a dollar or the three Rs. Take yer pick."

"Hey...I ain't losin' no wages," Gus exclaimed, startled. Gus had a very foggy idea of education. When he had made his radical declaration just now, it hadn't occurred to him that the move might cost him money.

Feeling vindicated again, Angus laughed at Hetty.

"What'd I tell you, Hetty King? These scoundrels live from hand to mouth. Ha, ha."

Certain he had squelched this meddling teacher, Angus turned on his heel and marched back towards the cannery, leaving Gus to deliberate his expensive choice. As Gus stood, riddled with doubt, Hetty saw her catch slipping away. She needed to do something fast to keep him on her hook.

"Angus, a word with you, if you don't mind."

Angus stopped at her call and waited suspiciously as Hetty hurried towards him.

"I'm ashamed of you, Angus McCorkadale," Hetty rapped out sternly. "I thought you were a God-fearing man."

Angus was taken aback by this sudden resort to religion and thought the tactic patently unfair.

"Don't you go dragging God into this," he ground out, hastily pulling his hat off and shooting a nervous glance heavenward.

"He's in it, whether you like it or not," Hetty declared, overriding anything else Angus might have been going to say. "This is charity we're discussing, man. Christian charity."

Hetty knew how to handle the Angus McCorkadales of the world. She paused only long enough for this resounding phrase to nail Angus to the spot before thundering on.

"Now, there's a boy who needs your help, a boy with gumption. He wants a chance to get some learning, Angus. Do your duty as a gentleman and a Presbyterian. Couldn't you split the shift?"

Despite his bluster, Angus was quite unequal to arguing duty and theology with the Avonlea schoolmistress, and he knew it. He shifted from foot to foot, twisted his hat brim and glanced uncomfortably at Gus. He might have learned enough reading and writing to run the cannery, but he was no match for the schoolteacher's debating skills.

"Oh, all right," he conceded sullenly, feeling that he was somehow being had but unable to figure out how. "I suppose he can take a shift before school and another after. But," he raised his voice so that everyone could hear, "if he can't handle it, he's fired."

Having snatched victory so narrowly from the jaws of defeat, Hetty now graciously shook Angus's hand.

"Well," she said in satisfaction, "it's settled."

She turned to Gus, who was now looking more than a little confused.

"I'll see you in school, Gus Pike. Eight-thirty sharp. Monday morning."

As Hetty walked off, looking pleased with herself, Pincher mimicked Hetty's voice and gestures, taking care, though, to make sure she was out of earshot.

"I'll see you in school, Gus Pike. Eight-thirty sharp."

Gus, instead of getting angry, only rapped Pincher playfully on the head, showing evidence of an easygoing nature that must have got him through many a rough spot in life.

"What do you know?" he exclaimed, more in wonder at the new state of his life than in answer to Pincher.

The other lads stood up too, for they had put in a hard day of work and wanted their suppers.

"Good luck, schoolboy," one of them said, half in fun, half as though he were faintly envious of Gus's courage in undertaking to better himself.

The boys walked off together leaving Gus still sitting on the dock. Gus took a long, contemplative puff on his pipe and gazed out to sea, as though already seeing new horizons for himself. The soft sea breeze played around him, and the cries of the gulls floated in the evening air. Yes, on such an evening, a lad might believe any possibility was real. Gus must have, for slowly, a huge, pleased smile spread across his face. He shook his head at the effect a couple of words to Hetty King had already had upon his settled ways of thinking.

Chapter Four

Despite the ridicule of his co-workers, Gus Pike kept to his resolve to get an education. Monday morning found him galloping across the fields towards the school, panting from the effort and sweating profusely. Inside, classes had already commenced with arithmetic drills. From the open windows, Gus could hear the children's voices floating outside as he approached.

"...two nines are eighteen, three nines are twenty-seven, four nines are thirty-six..."

Sara Stanley was doing the reciting, along with her cousins, Felicity and Felix King. Behind them, the younger children applied themselves silently to their workbooks.

"...five nines are forty-five, six nines are..."

Hetty, listening intently to the drills, suddenly rapped Felix on the knuckles with her pointer.

"Uh-uh, Felix, no counting with your fingers."

Guiltily, Felix snatched his fingers back. At eleven, Felix was a sturdy boy who had little inclination to scholarship. In fact, had he been able to get away with it, he would gladly have abandoned the joys of education altogether and gone to work with his father on the farm.

"I wasn't. They were moving by themselves," he protested unconvincingly.

Hetty flung him a skeptical look and turned to the rest of the children. She was pleased with the times tables and pleased with how well all the children had managed to learn under her tutelage. Avonlea arithmetic was one place, at least, where Muriel Stacey would be hard put to find fault.

"Very good, class. Well now, let's practice, shall we, for the Lieutenant Governor's reception—"

At that moment, the door flew open and Gus Pike burst in, completely out of breath. Nevertheless, his eyes shone with anticipation from under the shock of dark, unruly hair that stood up in uncombed spikes around his head, and he grinned from ear to ear. He had shown up for his education equipped with a pipe in one hand, a fiddle under his arm and bare feet horny as leather from a total lack of acquaintance with shoes.

"Whew! Run the whole way! Sweatin' like a pig."

Felix erupted into a giggle, then shut his mouth quickly as Hetty turned to the new arrival. One did not mention "sweat" in Hetty's class, much less dare to be unpunctual. Her eyebrows shot up ominously.

"Children...I believe you know Gus Pike, who's managed to be late on his very first day of school."

"I told ya, I run my guts out," Gus repeated, determined not to be found wanting this early in the learning game.

The whole classroom tittered, making Hetty decide she had better start polishing this rough diamond as soon as possible. What if Muriel Stacey had been hovering around to hear the boy talk like that!

"A person's 'guts' do not 'run,' Gus," Hetty informed the boy reprovingly.

"Felt like guts runnin' out to me, Miss," Gus answered cheerfully, failing to get Hetty's point and provoking another spate of snickers.

Hetty pursed her lips tight and tried another angle. After all, you couldn't scold a boy for breaking the rules if he didn't know what the rules were in the first place.

"In my school, punctuality is...is..."

Hetty's words died in horror as Gus nonchalantly struck a match against a desk to light his pipe. He meant to be as comfortable as possible at this schooling business, and he didn't notice Hetty's disbelief until she began to sputter like a wet firecracker.

"Get rid of that...that disgusting..."

Hetty actually made a violent gesture at the pipe, causing Gus to rear back in surprise. Since he'd been a little nipper, puffing away like a chimney, no one had ever objected to him smoking.

"But I just lit up," he protested, unable to believe anyone could expect him to waste a fresh pipeful of tobacco.

"Put it out," Hetty commanded, beginning to look livid. "There's no smoking allowed in this school. And that fiddle. What did you bring that for?"

With great reluctance, Gus extinguished his pipe with his thumb and then lifted his fiddle lovingly. It was an old fiddle, one that had seen much use. It was covered in nicks and scratches and was very dark on the tip where it fitted under the chin to be played. Nevertheless, its varnish shone a rich gold from constant polishing, and Gus handled it so protectively that no harm could possibly have come to it, even if it had been constructed of eggshells. When he looked down at it, his whole expression softened and changed.

"This here fiddle goes where I go, even to the outhouse."

Snuffles and croaks echoed through the air as the entire schoolroom struggled to choke back mirth. Hetty stood aghast, for the outhouse was an even worse unmentionable than sweat in Hetty's class. She thumped her desk roundly with her pointer in an attempt to restore order.

"That is a phrase we do not use here. And the fiddle stays at home. Understand?"

Cavalier about his pipe he might be, but the fiddle was obviously something precious to Gus. At Hetty's order, he clutched the instrument to his chest and looked so shocked that even Hetty had to relent. She pointed out an empty desk and started towards Gus, as though she didn't trust him to seat himself without being personally conducted.

"All right, then, over here. Smartly, now. Over here."

As Hetty arrived where Gus was standing, she screeched to a halt and recoiled sharply, her face twisted in revulsion.

"Ooh! You reek of fish, boy. Kindly change your clothes before you come to school."

Well, well! School was certainly turning out to be full of queer surprises. Here Gus wasn't even sitting down yet and the teacher was taking exception to the very shirt on his back.

"I ain't got no other clothes," Gus told her stoutly. At the cannery, one set of clothes was quite enough for anybody so why would a fellow go to the trouble of toting about two?

Hetty, who had never heard of such a thing,

was again appalled. She looked Gus up and down, taking in his frayed, faded old shirt with the collar long ago torn away. The shirt resided under an old brown vest with one button left and an equally ancient jacket, with no buttons at all. The whole of this outfit, including what passed as trousers, was ornamented all over with greasy stains, torn at elbow and cuff and glistening where the ever-present fish scales had dried onto the fabric in patches. The clothes spoke volumes about the kind of hard, solitary, knockabout life Gus must have lived until then.

"Do you ever wash those?"

"Every Christmas, regular as clockwork," replied Gus proudly, confident this finicky teacher couldn't fault him on personal hygiene, at least.

The children could contain themselves no longer. Rules or no rules, they all erupted openly into laughter, and Hetty didn't even try to stop them. Seeing what a truly big job she had taken on with Gus, she only sighed.

"I see. Well, stand up straight then," she told him. "Pay attention. Let's see what you do know." Hetty rubbed at her nose with her handkerchief against the fishy odor as she tried to get back to school matters. "Can you read?"

"Nope. I figured you'd learn me readin' this mornin' and writin' by quittin' time."

As he stood ducking his head to Hetty, Gus kept glancing and grinning at the rest of the children, who were enjoying the show immensely. In fact, Gus was lapping up all the attention he was getting, even as Hetty let out a sniff of disbelief.

"Expected to learn everything in one day, did you?"

"Yep," Gus said complacently, fully expecting to get his education under his belt quickly so he could get back to his paying job at the cannery.

"That's most admirable, Gus," Hetty told him with asperity. "However, you'll find it takes much longer than a day. Well then, sit down over there behind Felix."

Gus sauntered over to the desk directly behind Felix and plopped himself down in it. Having never been in a schoolhouse before, Gus's only idea of how to act was taken from his rough companions in the bunkhouse.

"Hey, Felix," he drawled by way of greeting, for he and Felix had done some fishing together when Gus had been staying in the King barn. In fact, Felix had been properly flummoxed to see Gus pick up his bow beside the water and fairly fiddle the trout into biting the bait. However, Gus had smelt like a nice, fresh hayloft when he had stayed with the Kings. Now the fragrance of the cannery hit Felix like a wallop in the face with a wet cod. He reeled back with exaggerated reaction and made a face that almost set the class off again into titters and giggles. Hetty pointed to one of his nearby class-mates.

"Open the window, Tyler...wide. We will start from the beginning then." She looked significantly at her new pupil. "Look at this, Gus, please."

Hetty turned to the blackboard and wrote, in large letters, "G-U-S P-I-K-E." Gus cocked his head and looked at it, one eye squinting quizzically and then the other.

"What's that?" he inquired about the incompre-hensible squiggles.

"It's your name."

This had all the effect upon Gus that Hetty could have wanted. Gone instantly was the humorous slouch Gus had adopted. The lad sobered and his eyes popped as wide as if Hetty King had pulled a jackrabbit out of her ear.

"My name! No guff...that's my name?"

"It is," Hetty assured him, quelling the amuse-ment of the rest of the room with a severe glance. "And you can start to learn to print it by copying these letters, in order, over and over again on this slate. Here's your chalk. And don't stop until I say so. For the rest of you, let's recommence with the rehearsal of our poem, 'Breathes there a man...' All together now."

Gus took the slate and the chalk from Hetty. After a moment of awkward struggle with the unfamiliar implements, Gus got the slate right side up on the top of his desk and the chalk gripped resolutely in his fist. There was, underneath all the grins, a burning desire to learn—the same desire that had caused him to brave the jeers of his buddies and come racing through the early morning dew to the Avonlea school. Utterly oblivious to the rest of the room, he began, earnestly and laboriously, copying the strange-looking lines from the blackboard that somehow, by some powerful sorcery Gus meant to discover, spelled his own name.

It took some time for him to get "G-U-S P-I-K-E" down the first time. Even though the letters reeled and tilted and all but fell off the edge of the slate, Gus sat back and regarded the result of his handiwork quite transfixed by awe. All around him the children droned on with the dreary poem they were practicing for the Lieutenant Governor.

"Breathes there a man with a soul so dead,
Who never to himself hath said,
'This is my home...'"

Gus looked up at Hetty, holding up his slate for her to see the letters he had just printed. When he caught her eye, he smiled at her and nodded, very pleased with himself. Hetty, who had been trying to keep time with the poem, unbent enough to give him a small smile and a nod back, for not even Hetty King could resist the state of wondering delight into which those few scrawled letters had thrown the boy.

Gus bent over his slate and happily began copying his name all over again, his hand already less shaky, his resolve more firm. In spite of her strange aversion to pipes and guts and nice, ripe, fishy stinks, Hetty King had just handed Gus a magical key to a world hitherto closed to him. In Gus's mind, his new teacher had just assumed the stature of a minor divinity. If Hetty King could write his name out for him, just like that, why, she must know about everything else there is to know. And if she knew all that, how could she do any wrong?

Chapter Five

Gus spent a very happy morning copying and recopying his name. Sometimes the letters reeled drunkenly to the left and the right. Sometimes they were so tall and skinny as to be scarcely recognizable. Sometimes they were fat, squashy forms pushing each other rudely against the frame of the slate. Though Gus, as yet, had no idea of their individual significance, he admired the collected effect so much that he couldn't stop smiling to himself as his chalk squeaked and scraped over the slate's smooth, dark surface.

Gus was so pleased with himself that when recess was called, he snatched up his fiddle, which had sat on his desk all morning, and raced outside with the rest of the children. He felt as merry and full of joy as the youngest of them, bursting with energy, in spite of his being so big and having already worked a shift at the cannery before setting out for school.

In fact, Gus felt like dancing. So, without even thinking about it, he tucked his fiddle under his chin and struck up a tune so bright and frolicsome that the other children all stopped what they were doing and rushed over, their eyes sparkling with surprise. Fiddle music in the schoolyard! Who could have imagined such a thing!

Gus laughed and winked over his bow, which was flying so fast the human eye could scarcely follow it. Felix and Sara clapped their hands in time to the lilting music, while Felicity, who was almost fourteen, seemed totally entranced. Felicity loved music, and the way this rough, ragged boy played was something wonderful to her. No wonder Gus took the instrument everywhere with him. The fiddle was simply a natural extension of himself, another voice to express what Gus couldn't say in words, a stretch of vibrating strings singing out the lad's delight at learning to spell his name.

Anyone who could play fiddle was bound to be popular in Prince Edward Island. Gus was used to audiences, and he certainly knew how to please them. Giving the captivated children another wink, Gus started leading them around in a circle, cavorting this way and that, playing all the time while his young followers jumped and skipped in time with the tune.

Left to herself inside the empty school, Hetty was feeling pleased, in her own starchy way. Despite the fact that the room now smelled like the inside of a trawler's hold, some real learning had just taken place. Hetty picked up the slate Gus had been using, looked at the arduously traced letters and smiled to herself. The little acorn of education had just been planted, and from little acorns grew mighty oaks.

The very vastness of Gus Pike's ignorance was a challenge to Hetty. He seemed a perceptive boy. If his eagerness could be made to last, then the born teacher in Hetty saw real possibilities for him. Yes, she thought briskly, just let Muriel Stacey see what Hetty King could do with raw material like Gus Pike!

Hetty was examining the slate so intently that she failed to notice the riotous fun in the schoolyard until the breeze veered, carrying the merry strains of a reel through the open window to her ears. Her head flew up, and she was greeted by a sight that made her drop the slate in sudden consternation. Outside, Gus had marched his line of youthful followers all around the yard and straight to the spot where some workmen had been doing repairs on the school. They had left, sitting on two sawhorses, a pile of newly cut boards. Gus, with his long legs, had hopped easily up onto the boards. At the exact moment Hetty looked, he was leading the rest of the children along them, swaying on the springy wood like tightrope walkers. With a gasp, Hetty rushed to the door.

"GUS PIKE! Stop that at once!" she shouted in her fiercest, most commanding voice. Gracious heavens above, how would she get all the children down again without someone's neck getting broken?

Unfortunately, the effect of Hetty's ringing order was not the one she'd hoped for. The fiddle squawked to a halt and all the children behind Gus bumped into each other. Young Cecily King was so startled by the shout that she lost her balance and stumbled sideways. For one awful moment her arms windmilled frantically while her little body slowly canted towards the schoolhouse. Then, losing her footing altogether, she let out a terrible shriek and tumbled down onto the ground below.

For several seconds there was nothing but a petrified silence as everyone stared at the girl sprawled out on the grass. Then Hetty, Sara and Felicity raced to Cecily's side while the other children did their best to get off the boards without ending up in a heap beside their classmate.

Cecily's rescuers endured a moment of awful suspense as Cecily lay motionless and limp. Then, to the immense relief of all, she gave a grunt and a heave and struggled to sit up amidst the ring of worried faces. Aside from being dazed, shaken up and smudged with dirt, she was pretty much unharmed. Above her, Gus still balanced lightly on the boards, fiddle in hand, sobered and sheepish at the accident he supposed his music had caused.

"Cecily King, you could have knocked yourself senseless!" Hetty scolded, rebounding from the heart-stopping fright she had suffered at seeing Cecily's tumble. Hetty was prickly with relief that nothing worse than a shaking up had happened to a child for whom she was responsible. Following a pied piper about in her schoolyard, indeed!

Felicity, seeing that Cecily was quite all right, hastily stood her sister up and dusted her off. Despite the accident, Felicity was still enthralled with the music and felt the rhythm of the tune lingering inside her. Besides, she knew exactly whom her aunt would be angry with next, and she wanted to save him.

Felicity, usually so dainty and particular in her manners, had a soft spot for Gus. And perhaps the soft spot could be explained by Gus's part in a certain embarrassing adventure Felicity had involved herself in while Gus had been staying at the farm. Determined to go to her first grown-up dance, Felicity had sneaked out of the house one night, directly against her parents' express orders. Seeing that she wasn't to be dissuaded, Gus volunteered to see her safely along the road. And when Alec King finally stormed into the dance in search of his disobedient daughter, Gus did his best to save her from her father's wrath. Though Felicity was brought home in disgrace, she still felt grateful to Gus for his efforts.

"Aunt Hetty," she breathed, seeing the thunderclouds in her aunt's face and determined to defend the musician, "did you hear Gus? Doesn't he play beautifully?"

Hetty hadn't exactly been listening to the fine points of Gus's performance, and, in any case, she wasn't known for her musical ear. On top of that, she certainly did not approve of music in the midst of a school day, especially when it led her charges into the way of mischief and bodily harm. She stood up abruptly, shaking out her skirt.

"Wild and foolish behavior, all of you," she reprimanded. "Thank the Lord Muriel Stacey wasn't here to witness this performance. She'd have had a conniption fit."

Hetty glared at Gus, who, as oldest pupil in the school, ought to have known better, even if he hadn't yet been there a full day.

"And as for you, Gus Pike, I won't put up with these shenanigans. Never bring that fiddle into my school again. Never!"

The force of this last command seemed to relieve some of Hetty's built-up anxiety. She took a deep breath and turned to the rest of the miscreants. They shifted uneasily under her eye, wondering if they were in for a chewing-out too.

"All right, then. You may resume playing," was all Hetty said to them, having apparently vented the last of her vehemence upon Gus.

With this outburst of generosity, Hetty marched back into the school, leaving the children to stare from one to the other uneasily. Gus struggled to absorb this rude introduction to schoolyard decorum. It proved a hard lesson for him, and he stood for the longest time, holding his fiddle in drooping fingers, silent and chastised.

Chapter Six

The incident at recess made for a subdued, hard-working afternoon in the classroom, which was got through without further incident. Gus had put his fiddle aside quietly and toiled over his letters, looking so serious that Pincher and the fellows might have been hard put to recognize him. When school was finally dismissed for the day, all the children sped off in different directions towards home, leaving only Gus in the schoolroom with Hetty. Gus seemed reluctant to leave his slate; he kept glancing at it devotedly as he gathered up his precious fiddle and stuck his pipe between his teeth, ready to be lit up the moment he got out the door. As Hetty packed her basket with work to take home, Gus began to recite, quite absently, under his breath:

> *"Breathes there a man with a soul so dead,*
> *Who never to himself hath said,*
> *'This is my home, my native land,'*
> *Whose heart has ne'er within him burned..."*

Hetty stopped right in the middle of what she was doing and listened to Gus with startled curiosity. Quite unaware of Hetty's interest, Gus started for the door. Just as he stepped out, Hetty came to life.

"Gus Pike...Gus."

Tucking her basket over her arm, she followed him hastily outside, where Gus had come to an apprehensive halt.

"Gus Pike, I want a word with you."

Gus snatched his pipe from his teeth and jammed it into his breast pocket, unmindful of all the good tobacco spilling out.

"How'd you learn that poem?" Hetty demanded, gratified to see how quickly her new pupil had whipped the pipe out of sight.

Relieved that it was only the poem Hetty was interested in and not his clothes or his fiddle, Gus shrugged.

"It's in my head," he replied casually, as if he took it for granted that his head was full of all sorts of queer things, including poems overheard in schools.

"I beg your pardon?"

Gus pointed back to the classroom. "They was talkin', I was listenin'..."

To prove it, he sucked in a breath and launched into the rest of the poem, the doleful words all the more wildly incongruous for the ease with which they slipped off his tongue.

"As home his footsteps he had turned,
From wandering on a foreign strand.
If such there breathe

Go mark him well,
For him no minstrel raptures swell,
High—"

"Remarkable!" Hetty burst out, remembering all the labor she was going through to hammer those very same lines into the heads of the other children. "Quite, quite remarkable! With an ability like that, you could go a long way, young man!"

Hetty had been pleased with Gus's application to his copying all day, but she had not guessed such quick intelligence could reside in such a rough, unpolished boy. Now her eyes lit up with true animation. This was the equivalent, for a teacher, of stumbling over a great nugget of gold lying, all unsuspected, in a gravel heap.

"And I dare say," Hetty thought gleefully to herself about the fine raw material that had just fallen into her hands, "*that* will give Muriel Stacey something to chew on."

Just as Hetty began to get swept up in a dream of academic glory for her new *protegé*, however, Gus ruined the good impression he had just made by leaning over to pick at his toe, which was swollen and covered with grime. Hetty jerked out of her reverie and curled her lip in disgust.

"Don't pick your toes in front of me, boy," she barked in irritation.

Gus straightened and put his foot down gingerly. He was forever having to cope with splinters from the old floors at the cannery.

"Toe's full o' pus, Miss. Hurts like the devil."

All Hetty could do was sigh. Gus might have all kinds of ability, but the task of shaping it into something useful was starting to look too daunting even for her. She couldn't even be angry, for she saw that Gus truly thought he was doing nothing wrong.

"You have no conception of manners whatsoever, have you? No doubt about it—you'd need fixing from top to bottom to be a gentleman. I certainly don't have the time."

But even as Hetty started closing the school door behind her, Gus suddenly took a half step towards her from where he stood, his lips parted. Hetty had uttered another magic word for him: "gentleman." The same longing, the same blind drive towards betterment that had brought Gus, large as he was, to sit with little children in the schoolhouse, had been stirred again.

"I want to be a gen'leman, Miss, but..."

Hetty paused, her hand still on the school door, then turned, expectantly. Her look caused the rest of Gus's words to get stuck in his throat. He fell into an abashed silence, dropping his head and clutching his new notebook awkwardly.

Who could resist such open, yet thoroughly confused longing, such a craving for learning so sorely
in need of a guide? Hetty regarded Gus thoughtfully, then reached into her basket for a book. After a
moment's hesitation, for it was a rather valuable
book, she held it out to the boy.

"Well, I...yes. This book belonged to my father,
Isaiah King. It's mostly drawings, so.... It's called
How to Be a Gentleman."

The book was a fat little volume with a dark
calfskin cover and a look of containing enough
information to split a poor fellow's head. Tucking
his fiddle under his arm, Gus took the book cau-
tiously, as though it might be hot, and opened it
with immense curiosity. From the flickers of awe on
his face, one might suppose he had just been
handed the secrets of the ages all bound up into a
handy, portable volume.

Unfortunately, the first picture the book fell
open to was that of a dandified fellow in a top hat
lifting a teacup to his lips. He held the cup with his
pinky finger raised foppishly and his lips puckered
in readiness, somewhat like a prune. Gus eyed the
man's pose in puzzlement.

"What's his finger stuck out in the air for?"

"Well, that's how a proper gentleman holds his
teacup," Hetty explained, even though she herself
had a low opinion of men who drank their tea this

silly way. "This book shows you how to dress properly, how to comb your hair, how to greet people in public."

But, of all the gentlemanly skills to be learned, Gus was most intrigued with the raised pinky finger. He creased the book open to that page and studied it. He flared his nostrils just like the dandy in the picture and raised his own pinky finger in an unconsciously ridiculous imitation.

Hetty glanced at him in despair. "Well, Rome wasn't built in a day, to be sure," she sighed.

Hetty closed the door of the schoolhouse behind her and hitched her basket before setting out for Rose Cottage.

"Well, take the book with you," she told Gus. "Study the pictures. Perhaps something will rub off on you. Of course, I will help you, Gus, as much as I'm able," she added, really meaning it. "In fact, since we're both going the same way..." She pointed towards the road before them. "Perhaps we could walk along together for a while."

Gus realized he was actually being asked to escort the teacher home. Immediately, he forgot all about the raised pinky and beamed from ear to ear.

"Yes, Miss...Miss King," he got out, managing, for the first time, to address Hetty properly.

"Yes," Hetty confirmed, pleased at this new leap in progress.

Pretending Gus was a gentleman already, she took his arm as a proper lady should. The two nodded to each other in exaggerated politeness and set out jauntily along the grassy track.

Hetty wasn't about to miss any opportunity to further Gus's education. She couldn't waste a second if she expected to whip him into shape in time to impress Muriel Stacey. She declaimed at length on the subject of manners and propriety, while Gus clutched his fiddle and his book under one arm, supported Hetty with the other and bent his head deferentially to catch every golden word Hetty had to say. In Gus's eyes, Hetty was growing more illustrious by the minute. Any woman who would give him a book on how to be a gentleman and teach him to copy out his own name in the span of a single day had to be in regular communion with higher powers than Gus had yet been able to dream of.

"Mark my words, boy, you'll never regret coming to school," Hetty promised expansively. "Reading and writing and arithmetic...why, they're all one needs, really, to get through life."

Hetty paused to let these gems sink in. Then, casting a sidelong glance at Gus to see how he was taking it, she decided to probe a little further into the life of this unusual lad. Much as she disapproved of all the gossip in the general store, especially if it were about herself, Hetty was not without her own share of curiosity. Besides, wasn't it her duty to find out all she could about those whose education was entrusted to her care?

"I don't suppose your...people...are educated?"

"Ain't got no people," Gus informed her.

As the head of the King clan, a family that could trace its ancestors back several generations, Hetty found it hard to imagine such a state. She waved her free hand.

"Don't be silly. Everyone has relatives of some sort."

"My mother's dead."

"Gracious!" Hetty was taken aback by this blunt confession and almost stumbled over a tuft of grass. Poor lad!

"I'm very sorry to hear it. Was it sudden?"

"Yep. My father busted her heart."

Hetty's mouth dropped open and polite words failed her entirely.

"He...how did he do that?" she exclaimed with most unladylike fascination.

"Got sent to prison," said Gus, supporting Hetty's elbow to keep her walking straight along the road.

"Prison!"

Gus had now managed to horrify Hetty King almost to her bones, and he nonchalantly proceeded to double the effect.

"Yep. Kilt a fella. Whacked his head open with an ax."

Hetty came to a halt and all but dropped her basket into the ditch.

"Your father's a murderer?" she asked in a strangled whisper.

"He weren't no gen'leman, Miss," Gus grinned. And before Hetty could stammer out anything else, he spun on his heel. "Well, better get goin' to work. Gonna get heck. See you tomorrow."

Giving Hetty a comradely thump on the shoulder, Gus flung round and set off at a run over the hill in the direction of the cannery, leaving Hetty aghast at the Rose Cottage gate. When he turned to wave, just before disappearing into the brush that marked the edge of the pasture, she was still standing there, fluttering her fingers weakly and trying to absorb the shock.

Gus reached the cannery just in the nick of time for his shift. Under the glowering eye of Angus McCorkadale, who was watching closely to see whether education had ruined Gus's ability to lug boxes, Gus sweated and labored through the long hours.

When his shift was finally over, Gus wasn't interested in rest. In fact, he could hardly wait to get back to his notebook and practice what he had learned that day. While the other workers built a bonfire outside the cannery and lounged in its light, laughing and joking, Gus bent over his notebook, copying and recopying his name. All the while, he drank from his chipped mug of tea with his pinky finger extended. Pincher, suspicious of his friend's silence, came over and gave Gus a poke on the shoulder. Gus laughed and tilted his notebook so Pincher could see. "Betcha don't know what this is," Gus challenged, waving his work under Pincher's nose.

Pincher gave a rude grunt and pushed his hat further forward over his matted curls. "Bunch of chicken scratching, ya ask me," he commented disparagingly, his sneer expressing his complete scorn for anything he couldn't understand.

Gus laughed again, triumphantly. "It's my name," he crowed, bursting with pride at his accomplishment.

"Yer name? Well, who cares about yer name?"

To show his disdain, Pincher made an idle grab at the gentleman's book lying nearby. Gus snatched it back from Pincher's grubby paws.

"Get yer hands off that!'

"Give us a tune, Gus," Pincher demanded, for Gus had been the main source of nightly entertainment in the bunkhouse. It was very boring to have him silently scratching away in some notebook.

"I've got better things to do," Gus tossed back, returning to his homework. Hetty had told him he must spend every spare moment he could practicing his letters.

"Afraid of what the teacher will say?" Pincher taunted him, leaning over his shoulder. "Give us a tune."

Defiantly, Pincher twanged a string on Gus's precious fiddle, which was propped at Gus's elbow. Even as Gus moved to defend it, Pincher grabbed up the instrument and waved it about just out of Gus's reach.

"Come on, I dare you," Pincher mocked, wagging his head and grinning his toothy grin.

"Yeah, come on!" the other lads chimed in, jumping up from the boxes and stomping their feet in the dust.

Pincher plinked the fiddle string again. Instantly, Gus sprang to his feet and seized the fiddle back. Pincher danced out of reach, and the rest of the workers began to shout for music.

As Gus peered around at the circle of firelit faces, the memory of all the other riotous evenings in this same spot came flooding back. His toes wanted to dance and his fingers longed to fly over the strings, but his head and heart wanted to practice writing. For the first time, Gus was feeling the split between the world he belonged to and the new world he wanted to join. The shouts around him increased. Confused and angered by all these conflicting demands, Gus flung his fiddle to his chin and struck the bow across it.

The moment the first notes sang out, everyone started dancing and clapping. Gus launched into a reel. Its lilting rhythm carried away his anger, for Gus loved his music far too much to resist its temptation long. As the jigs and dances spun from his flying fingers, everyone, men and women alike, began to whirl and leap. Music had the power to wipe away the hard toil of the day and drop an hour or two of forgetful laughter into the drudgery of their lives. Gus, too, forgot everything but the fun he was having. He played on and on until the dancers dropped from exhaustion. Gus himself ended up fast asleep by the dying embers, his fiddle cradled lovingly in his arms and his homework long ago kicked aside, lying unnoticed on the ground.

Chapter Seven

The revelries at the cannery roared late into the night—so late that, when the boys were shaken awake to work the morning shift, they stumbled blearily about, sure they had got only a few winks of sleep. The episode did nothing at all for Gus's punctuality at school. As before, he was seen thumping across the fields, shirttail flapping behind him, in a vain attempt to get to school before Hetty rang the bell and shut the door.

As he thudded into the schoolyard, he found the door shut tight and not even the sound of times tables floating on the morning air to mask his late arrival. To his left, where the workmen's boards still rested on the sawhorses, he was greeted by the man who was doing the construction in the yard. Gus managed to silence the fellow with a gesture before he could actually call out and give Gus's lateness away. What's more, Gus, against Hetty's orders, was again clutching his fiddle under his arm.

Inside the school, the class was working quietly at their assignments. Gus opened the door, sneaked inside and tried to slide into his desk unnoticed. He soon learned what all the other schoolchildren knew already—that teachers have eyes in the backs of their heads. Without even looking up from her own work, Hetty knew Gus had arrived.

"You're late," she said grimly. "And what's more…" She lifted her head and frowned. "I told you to leave that fiddle at home."

"I forgot," Gus panted, trying to cram his long legs under the low desk. That his excuse was true didn't make it sound any less lame.

Gus had caught Hetty in a less than accommodating mood. She could forgive a pupil for not knowing the rules, but once the rules had been explained, she saw no need to allow violations without consequences to the guilty party. Her gaze swept over Gus austerely, taking in every detail.

"You forgot. My, my. It appears you forgot your homework, as well. Where's your notebook?"

Gus gave a little start, for he just now remembered the notebook lying open and abandoned by the ashes of last night's bonfire. This business of being a scholar was a lot more complicated than he had imagined.

"Aw, the other fellas were drinkin', see..."

"Drinking?" Hetty shot straight up out of her chair. Drinking! Mentioned openly by a pupil in her classroom! This wasn't a thing Hetty was used to dealing with among the pliable, well-behaved children of Avonlea. She stood rigid as Gus hurried to try to save himself.

"I played a tune, ya see. I must have snoozed off." Which shouldn't have been any wonder, what with Gus working a split shift, going to school, playing the fiddle at night and puzzling over how to be a gentleman besides.

Hetty's mouth became a thin, offended line.

"Fiddling, smoking! I suppose your father did all those things, as well?"

If she hoped to quell Gus with that reference, she was sadly mistaken. He sat up straight and started to grin.

"My father? He didn't do anything else. 'Cept women. He runned with women. One, her hair was red as flame. You should'a—"

"Gus Pike, that's quite enough!" Hetty exploded, cutting him off before he could spill yet more appalling revelations into the ears of all the fascinated schoolchildren. "I see this calls for a complete change of attitude."

Her gaze fell on the fiddle, which seemed to be the instigator of all Gus's wayward behavior. Before Gus could blink, Hetty had marched over to his desk and snatched the instrument up.

"I am confiscating this, Gus. No more fiddle."

An instant later, the fiddle was put inside the tall white cupboard beside the front desk, and Hetty was firmly closing the door.

Gus sat staring. "But that's mine," he protested in alarm and disbelief. Beyond his pipe and the few clothes on his back, that fiddle was the single possession Gus Pike owned. He valued it almost more than one of his own arms.

Hetty was unmoved by the dismay paralyzing Gus. Once she had decided about a thing, there was no turning back. Gus had lived a pretty footloose life so far. She meant to see that he learned some discipline now.

"It stands in the way of learning. You want to learn, don't you?"

She had Gus there. Gus twisted at his cuff.

"Yes, but—"

"No buts. I can't educate you if you persistently indulge in this foolishness."

As the awful price of book-learning began to register on Gus, he started up in his seat.

"But...I love my music!"

This heartfelt protest sprang from the bottom of Gus's soul. From as far back as he could remember, there had always been the lilting cadences of the fiddle, first from his father's hands, then from his own. Music was the one beautiful thing in Gus's knocked-about young life and was exceedingly dear to him. How would he ever have got through the loss of his mother without his fiddle to comfort him? How would he stand all the long nights around the cannery without a dance and a tune? That old fiddle could practically talk all by itself; it could say all the things Gus could not imagine putting into words. Why, if he couldn't have his music, he felt he would simply burst.

Hetty was not impressed. Determined to save the boy from frittering himself away on foolishness, she did not read the plea on the lad's stricken face.

"It doesn't love you, Gus," she told him briskly. "It's a bad habit. Do you want to read and write?

❧❧❧

"And the fiddle stays at home. Understand?"
Cavalier about his pipe he might be, but the
fiddle was obviously something precious to him.
At Hetty's order, he clutched the instrument
to his chest and looked so shocked
that even Hetty had to relent.

❧❧❧❧❧

When his shift was finally over,
Gus wasn't interested in rest. In fact,
he could hardly wait to get back to his notebook
and practice what he had learned that day.

❦❦❦

"You're lucky it's only a muscle strain,"
Dr. Blair informed Hetty,
who had hardly been a model of cooperation
while he had examined her and then spooned
a bracing mixture down her throat.

❧

"And now, Your Excellency, Mrs. Vaughn."
She nodded towards the appropriate dignitaries.
"With your kind permission,
I would like to request that the assembly
please remain seated. The pupils of Avonlea school
have prepared a special tribute to someone
whom they greatly respect and admire."

Do you want to get somewhere in this world? Or do you want to wreck your life and end up in the gutter?"

What could an unlettered lad answer to that? Gus sank back into his seat again while, all around, the rest of the children sat still as church mice. Pressing her advantage, Hetty drew herself up to her full height and turned on the full power and authority of her position. She was the one who held the keys to the gates of learning and, no matter what she said, in Gus's eyes it was the truth.

Unfortunately, Hetty chose just this moment to turn melodramatic.

"I see where the danger lurks," she admonished darkly, staring so hard at Gus that she looked as though she could read his inmost wayward thoughts. "It's in your very soul. Do you hear me?"

Gus actually turned pale at her words and wondered how he could have stumbled so blindly through his life without seeing the dangers snapping at him all around. He was a lad of deep feeling who had had precious little attention paid to him. What's more, he was full of strange beliefs picked up as he wandered about from one job to the next. He took Hetty King's words to heart and believed them, every one.

Seeing Gus quelled into silence and obedience, Hetty sailed magnificently back to her desk and sat down again. The whole room went back to work, Gus along with it, though he couldn't help frequent glances at the cupboard where his fiddle was imprisoned.

Hetty gave him plenty to do. She even sent him outside at lunchtime to hunch over a word list while the rest of the children dashed about at play. Presently, Hetty herself came out into the sunny schoolyard carrying her basket.

"Sara!" she called out.

Sara, who had been chasing a kite, sped over for her share of the lunch that had been packed that morning at Rose Cottage. Taking out a sandwich and handing Sara the basket, Hetty walked over to where Gus leaned on the workman's wagon, filling his notebook up with page after page of carefully copied words.

"All right, Gus," Hetty said magnanimously. "You can take five minutes to eat your lunch."

Packed lunches were another luxury unknown to Gus. He cast a hungry glance at the sandwich in Hetty's hand.

"Ain't brought none, Miss."

Sighing, Hetty divided her sandwich in half and held a part out to Gus. She was not going to have pupils going hungry in her schoolyard.

"You may share mine, then."

Wordlessly, Gus took the sandwich and swung it towards his mouth. It was thick ham on Olivia's fresh, home-baked bread, and Gus was eager to get it down in case Hetty changed her mind. Hetty stopped him with a gesture.

"Ah-ah. Didn't you forget something?"

Gus was caught with his jaws open wide and his tonsils hanging on view. Nevertheless, he paused to ponder, hitting upon the answer directly.

"Thank you, Miss King," he said, with a sudden grin at his own fine manners.

Social niceties taken care of, Gus then wolfed down a huge hunk of the sandwich, swallowed noisily and finished off with a burp that practically rattled the wagon wheels.

Hetty shuddered.

"That may be the way they eat in the cannery," she said, looking pained. "But a gentleman takes a small bite."

By way of demonstration, Hetty took a diminutive bite from the sandwich half she held in her hand and chewed it daintily. After a moment, Gus realized he could relax; he wasn't in competition with ravenous fellows like Pincher for the meal the cannery cooks provided. Extending his pinky exactly the way Hetty had done, Gus imitated her by taking a tiny bite too. Hetty carefully finished chewing and swallowed before continuing her speech.

"Chew it ten times," she instructed, "then swallow without gulping. Remember that when next you eat with those hooligans. You're different than they are now."

Different! Gus went still for a moment, and his face changed as this idea sank in, for if Hetty said it, Gus believed it. Hetty smiled approvingly as she and Gus ate the rest of their sandwich in silence. Gus chewed each delicate bite ten times, exactly as Hetty had shown him, beaming to himself over his speedy progress in the ways of polite society.

When school was dismissed, Felix, Felicity and Sara walked with Gus in the direction of the cannery. Felix hiked along at Gus's side, whacking at the heads of the tall grass as he went.

"I don't understand you," Felix said to Gus. "I hate going to school, but Mother and Father force me. Nobody forces you, and you go anyway. How come?"

"Because he's concerned about his future, Felix," Sara cut in as she contemplated that very subject. There was no limit to what an enterprising lad with a bit of reading and writing might do, she thought. Her busy imagination soared. "Maybe you could own a cannery someday, Gus, or a ship. Aunt Hetty says you have 'natural intellect.'"

"Or you could be a musician," cried Felicity, remembering how Gus's fiddle could cheer the whole world up. "You play beautifully. What do you think you want to do, Gus?"

Gus chewed his lip as he swung along, bereft of his fiddle tonight and carrying only his notebook. This wasn't a question anyone had ever bothered to ask him before. He got ready to speak, and then his cheeks reddened a bit.

"Aw, nothin'. It's stupid."

Of course, an answer like this only roused everybody's curiosity.

"Come on. Tell us," begged Felicity.

"We won't laugh," put in Felix. "Promise."

Despite his reluctance, Gus had evidently been wanting to tell his dreams to someone, for he finally said in a burst, "I want what you got."

"Us?" croaked Felix in surprise. "We don't have anything..."

"You got lots. You got people."

"A family?" Sara exclaimed. "You want a family?"

The color under Gus's tan grew even redder and he waved his notebook in the air.

"Aw, forget it. I tol' ya it was stupid."

Escaping from further discussion, Gus suddenly grinned his familiar grin and raced off ahead to work, leaving Sara, Felicity and Felix standing in the road.

"You really are strange," Felix shouted after him. "I want to get rid of my family."

"Felix!" Felicity glared at her brother reprovingly. She was his sister, after all, and didn't fancy being thought of as one of the annoyances he wanted to get rid of.

Sighing at the lot of them, Sara turned away and started walking again towards Rose Cottage, where her supper waited. Perhaps, having lost her own mother and father, she could understand a bit better what Gus meant. One of the advantages of having "people," she thought, was a regular, home-cooked meal every night.

Chapter Eight

Finally, the day Hetty had been dreading arrived—the day of Muriel Stacey's visit to Avonlea. Determined to do right by her longtime rival, Hetty had stuck fast to the privilege of serving Miss Stacey her first dinner in the neighborhood. As a consequence, Rose Cottage was thrown into an uproar with Hetty's preparations.

Hetty, abetted by Olivia and Sara, had slaved grimly all day, determined that no fault be found with any dinner served on the premises. In the kitchen, every pot the house possessed seemed to be bubbling and boiling on the stove, while Hetty popped from one to another of them, stirring the contents in turn and frowning fiercely as she took critical tastes. Not only were the pots bubbling, but three plump fruit pies were turning golden in the oven and a fat chicken was sizzling in the roasting pan, on its way to mouth-watering perfection. In the waves of heat given off by the roaring cast-iron cook stove, Olivia and Sara rushed about doing their best to help, even though nothing, on this day of days, seemed to satisfy Hetty.

"Put those flowers on the table, Sara," Hetty called out, trying distractedly to supervise the setting of the dining table. There had already been heated discussions over which set of good china to use, which flowers to pick and how they should be arranged. Olivia and Sara considered themselves the artistic souls in the house, while Hetty was the one who had read the book on flower arranging.

"Aunt Hetty," Sara asked, with atrocious timing, "could Miss Stacey really fire you if she felt like it?"

"Oh, heavens, Sara, she wouldn't do a thing like that," Olivia exclaimed, horrified at the very idea, and horrified that Sara should bring up the subject at a time like this.

Hetty had worked herself up into such a state of nerves and anxiety that she could almost imagine Muriel Stacey arriving with her own guillotine. She didn't agree with Olivia at all and jerked her head in that vehement way she had when she was truly agitated.

"Oh, wouldn't she, though! That woman's just

itching to write up a bad report. I know it."

Hetty all but burnt her tongue testing a sauce, then noticed Olivia and Sara surreptitiously re-arranging the flowers yet again. She flew from the stove to the table, which was set with all the splendor Rose Cottage could produce.

"Don't put the flowers there, Sara! No, not that way, Olivia! Not like that! For heaven's sake!"

Sara dropped the daisy she had been sliding into the vase and hurriedly stepped out of her aunt's way.

"You seem awfully nervous, Aunt Hetty," Sara commented, keeping a prudent distance.

Hetty brandished the heavy wooden spoon she was carrying and sucked in a breath. Long strands of hair had worked loose from her bun and her apron was twisted askew.

"Me? Why I'm cool as a cucumber. Now, if you two will kindly leave me and go pick up Muriel Stacey at the Biggins's, I shall quickly bathe myself—in peace and quiet."

Uncertain that Hetty had all the simmering pots and the elaborate dinner preparations under control, Olivia and Sara exchanged worried glances. Nevertheless, Miss Stacey had to be picked up from the boarding house. Rather too gladly, they made their escape from the kitchen and left on their mission.

After Sara and Olivia were safely on their way in

the buggy, Hetty cast a last look around the kitchen and betook herself to the bathhouse. The bathhouse was a rather rickety wooden affair standing against the outside wall of Rose Cottage. It contained a narrow tin bathtub and an overhead arrangement of bucket and cord which made it possible to have a shower. Over the closed door of the wooden structure, all that could be seen of Hetty was her head, carefully protected by a frilled cap. Soon her numerous petticoats were flung over the top of the door. Enjoying her moment of privacy, Hetty even hummed to herself while she gave a tug at the cord of the bucket. The cord was supposed to tip the bucket so that the heated water cascaded down. As if through sheer perversity, nothing but a trickle came out.

"Blasted thing!" Hetty sputtered. It was always on a day like this that things were bound and determined to go wrong.

She gave the cord another tug and then a mighty yank, this time so hard that the treacherous cord came right off the bucket as it finally tipped, spilling all the water at once. Hetty had applied all her strength to it, so when the rope snapped, she lost her balance and her feet flew out from under her. Down she went into the bathtub with a scream and an immense splash of water. She landed in the tub so hard that she stuck fast, with only her head above water and her hands waving helplessly about. No matter how she struggled, she could not get free again.

All unsuspecting, Sara and Olivia drove up in the buggy in the gathering dusk, with Miss Stacey sitting in state on the softest of the buggy seats and Sara gazing in admiration at this important personage from behind. Instead of the unforgiving monster Hetty had described, Miss Stacey had turned out to be a captivating, dimpled woman, full of smiles and pleasant manners. Where Hetty was gaunt and angular, Miss Stacey was all pretty curves and lively grace, with sparkling eyes, glossy, dark brown hair and smooth, fair skin. And on top of that, Miss Stacey knew about fashion, for she was dressed in the most elegant narrow-waisted outfit, complete with cording and ribbon and a jaunty little hat to match.

"Hetty made a wonderful dinner," Olivia was saying as she pulled up the horse and hurried to help Miss Stacey down.

Olivia, too, was on her best manners. She meant to do her bit for Hetty's career, even if it involved praising a hundred of Hetty's dinners. Olivia had just opened her mouth to extol the carrots when she was stopped cold by pathetic cries coming from the bathhouse. Cries, impossibly, in Hetty's voice.

"Help," wailed Hetty, sloshing about, "Heellllp! Somebody heeeeeelp!"

"What on earth?" cried Olivia, turning around. "That sounds like Hetty." She stepped through the gate and peered around the side of the house. "Hetty!" she called out in concern, "Hetty!"

Having finally ascertained the source of the cries, Olivia began to run towards the bathhouse, only to be frozen in her tracks by the sight of smoke seeping out of the kitchen window. Torn between one emergency and the next, Olivia hovered anxiously.

"Oh, Sara, run inside and see what's burning," she shouted frantically, even as she began to sprint towards the bathhouse again. "Hetty?"

As Sara raced into the house through the back door, Olivia reached the bathhouse and wrenched open the flimsy wooden door. There she found Hetty stuck in the tub, up to her neck in water and groping madly at a wet towel.

"M-my-my back...I can't move!" Hetty groaned, still struggling uselessly to get up. Her kicks sent yet another wave of water sloshing over onto the floor towards Olivia's best shoes.

To be caught this way by anyone was utterly humiliating for Hetty, but today, it seemed, the very worst fate must fall upon her. Twisting her head, she caught sight of Muriel Stacey, right on Olivia's heels, staring through the open bathhouse door.

"Hetty!" Miss Stacey cried out anxiously.

When Miss Stacey tried to crowd into the doorway too, Hetty went a little mad.

"Out!" she bellowed at Olivia. "Get her out!"

Olivia had time to do nothing, for at that moment, Sara came bolting out of the kitchen again.

"Aunt Olivia, Aunt Olivia, the dinner's on fire!" Sara shrieked at the top of her lungs, shaken by the sight of fruit pies flaring up in the oven and smoke billowing from the charred interiors of pots that had once held Hetty's finest vegetables and gravies.

But Olivia couldn't leave Hetty trapped in the tub. Why, she might drown of her own twisting about!

"Good Lord, Hetty, what happened?" Olivia demanded, trying with all her might to pull Hetty out by the shoulder.

Miss Stacey, who was not a cool-headed superintendent of schools for nothing, stepped into the fray.

"Olivia, you take one arm and I'll take the other. Sara, you'd better see to the stove. Are you in pain, Hetty?"

For answer, Miss Stacey got an ear-splitting yowl as the accident victim was jerked unceremoniously from the tub. Even then, Hetty received precious little attention from her rescuers, who hurriedly wrapped her in a towel and half-carried her round to the side door in a great hurry to help Sara in case the house was really on fire.

Fortunately, they found Sara tossing the smoking pots into the sink and dousing them with water from the pump. Once the fruit pies were extinguished and the little dancing flames on the chicken smothered, the kitchen proved to be unharmed. Luckily for Rose Cottage, cast-iron stoves do not catch fire, even when their entire contents belch black smoke and char themselves to cinders.

Hetty, still protesting at the top of her lungs, was wrapped in a blanket, propped up in a chair in the parlor and made to stay there while Dr. Blair was summoned to examine her. With Hetty being so stubborn, this, Olivia felt, was the only way to find out whether Hetty had actually broken anything or not.

"You're lucky it's only a muscle strain," Dr. Blair informed Hetty, who had hardly been a model of co-operation while he had examined her and then spooned a bracing mixture down her throat. The doctor straightened up and clicked his black bag shut. Hetty, wrapped from neck to toe in a gray blanket, peered malevolently at him from under the frill of her bath cap, which was still jammed damply over her head.

Meanwhile, Miss Stacey bustled in from the kitchen, one of Hetty's own aprons tied around her waist. So far, she hadn't had one moment to sit down and act the pampered guest. Instead, she was doing the very thing guaranteed to irritate Hetty the most: she was taking charge.

"Hetty, Sara's just scraped a few burnt bits off the chicken, and I'm gonna whip up a little savory. Supper should be just fine."

With her air of calm command, Miss Stacey looked as though she rescued people from bathtubs and magically repaired charred dinners every day. Before Hetty could reply, the doctor finished his prescription.

"I recommend at least five days total rest."

"Impossible, Doctor," Hetty exploded. "I have school to teach."

Just to show the doctor she had had enough of his foolishness, Hetty made to spring up out of the chair. Her strained back muscles would have none of it, and they stabbed at her all the way down to her tailbone. With a gasp, she plopped back down amongst the striped cushions.

"Oh, Hetty," said Miss Stacey reprovingly. "There, you see? How can you even think of teaching when you're in such terrible pain?"

Miss Stacey paused thoughtfully, and then her eyes lit up with enthusiasm.

"The solution is perfectly simple. I'll fill in for you."

Trapped, Hetty stared at her visitor. It was her worst nightmare come true. The last thing Hetty wanted was the superintendent of schools messing about on her own in Hetty's well-ordered classroom.

"No, you don't. You—you can't! I mean, you mustn't. It'll upset everything."

"Oh, piffle, Hetty," Miss Stacey scoffed. "Teaching school is just like riding a bicycle. Once you've done it, you never forget how."

Considering the arrangement fixed, Miss Stacey strode back towards the kitchen, leaving Hetty sputtering in bodily affliction and mental rage. Olivia, who had been hovering in the parlor door, clasped her hands in relief that at least one problem had been solved.

"Thank you, Miss Stacey," Olivia called after her, avoiding Hetty's killing looks. "I don't know what we would have done without you."

"I'm afraid rest is the only cure," the doctor added in the face of Hetty's intransigence. There was just a hint of satisfaction in his voice at being able to ground a patient who had proved so annoyingly troublesome.

Hetty moaned in pain and scowled fearfully at her younger sister. "Olivia!" she muttered between clenched teeth, making Olivia look very nervous indeed about the days ahead with Hetty shut up against her will in the house.

Chapter Nine

"Good morning, children," Miss Stacey sang out cheerfully the next morning to the assembled pupils of the Avonlea school. She had glided in just a few minutes earlier, taking everyone except Sara and the King children completely by surprise. Now she stood beside Hetty's desk and looked so at ease there that she might have been in charge of that same classroom all her life.

"For the benefit of those I haven't already met, my name is Miss Muriel Stacey," the new teacher announced.

"Good morning, Miss Stacey," the class chorused back in well-trained unison. They all sat primly in their desks, their darting glances and suppressed grins giving away their excitement at the arrival of this delightful-looking substitute for Hetty King.

Miss Stacey was smiling from under clouds of dark brown hair done up in fashionable rolls. Her blouse was full of exquisite little tucks and, over it, she wore a white shawl, hand-crocheted into lovely lacy patterns, about as pretty as anything the children had seen in Avonlea. Oh, this Miss Stacey promised to be a delight.

Not everyone, however, was riveted by the new arrival. At the very back, one head nodded in weariness, one set of eyelids drooped slowly shut. Gus Pike, who had contrived to be on time that morning, seemed to be paying a heavy price for his exertions. Dark circles lay under his eyes, and he periodically had to right himself as his body canted to one side or another, threatening to slide right out of his desk. When Miss Stacey introduced herself, Gus lifted his head and made a mighty effort to catch her name. Her voice floated to him as though from a long, long distance away as the struggle to stay awake grew too much for him. Finally, his lids fell shut, his head tipped forward, and he slumped, by almost imperceptible degrees, down in his desk.

"Please don't be alarmed," Miss Stacey continued, smiling even wider in reassurance lest the children think some dreadful disaster had overtaken their regular teacher. "Miss King took a rather nasty spill last night, and I'm just filling in for a few days, until she's made a complete recovery." Miss Stacey paused to let that news sink in before going on. "Filling the shoes of a teacher like Miss King is never an easy task, but let me assure you that I was a teacher for many, many years, and some of my happiest days were spent teaching right here in this classroom." She looked around fondly at the wooden desks and the familiar blackboard for a moment, then got down to business. "All right, everyone, gather those notebooks together. We're going to have a class outdoors this morning. Come along. Come along, now. Out you go."

A class outside! Actually outdoors!

A thrill of disbelief rippled through the children. This Miss Stacey had only been in the school for a few minutes, and already she was proposing something that would have given Hetty King a fit. The whole class jumped up, smiling. As fast as they could, they scrambled to grab their books and file out the door before the substitute changed her mind and the outing turned out to be too good to be true. Only when they were almost all out into the sunshine did the sound of snoring reverberate through the room. Turning round in surprise, Miss Stacey discovered Gus, limp as an old piece of ship's rope, his head in his arms, fast asleep.

The last three children remaining were Sara, Felix and Felicity. The snore caused Sara to frown, Felix to giggle and Felicity to leap once again to Gus's defense.

"Gus tires himself out, Miss Stacey," Felicity said by way of explanation. "He gets up at three in the morning to go to work at the cannery."

"Then he comes to school, works again after school and does homework, without anyone forcing him!" Felix added, expressing his amazement at such a prodigy. All the bribes in the world couldn't have forced Felix to do even half as much.

Where Hetty King might have rapped Gus with her pointer and ordered him to wake up, Miss Stacey only paused thoughtfully, taking in the youthful hands, already so work-hardened, and the relaxed face looking so vulnerable in sleep. Gus still wore his raggedy clothes but they seemed, sometime quite recently, to have actually been washed in water and had some of the fish stains pounded out of them. His shaggy hair showed signs of a comb and his sore toe was now bound up in a tidy rag. Whatever else he had been doing, Gus had been pouring over the book on how to be a gentleman.

"Oh dear. No wonder he's so exhausted. You three go on outside. I'll be along in just a moment. Go on, now."

Drawn by the bright day outside, the three children sped from the room to join the others. Miss Stacey, far from shaking her charge awake, simply took off her shawl, draped it warmly over Gus and left him to sleep.

For the rest of the children, though, Miss Stacey had more athletic things in mind. Arithmetic, she soon informed them, could be combined quite handily with physical exercise. Out in the schoolyard, she lined them up and started them doing touch-their-toes exercises in time to their multiplication tables. Notebooks and pencils were laid to one side as they counted off their twelve-times tables.

"...ten twelves are a hundred and twenty. Eleven twelves are a hundred and thirty-two. Twelve twelves are a hundred and forty-four."

Panting and glowing, they finished their exercises, amazed at how easily the multiplication tables danced off their tongues when their bodies moved in time and they were having fun. Miss Stacey applauded them.

"Excellent, just excellent."

Again doing something Hetty would never have dreamed of, she hoisted herself up to sit on the tailgate of the workman's wagon, her toes swinging just above the grass.

"Well, you certainly seem to have those multiplication tables down pat," she went on. "Now, what else have you been doing as part of the regular curriculum?"

Imitating their teacher, some of the children hopped up onto the boards still sitting on the sawhorses and ranged themselves in a row while the others sat down in front. Since they faced Miss Stacey, the whole arrangement formed a sort of ready-made classroom.

"Well," Sara began, "we've mostly been getting ready for the Lieutenant Governor's reception. We're reciting a poem that Aunt Hetty picked out."

"May I hear it?"

Sara rolled her eyes at the others, stood up and began to recite.

"Breathes there a man with soul so dead,
Who never to himself hath said,
'This is my home, my native land,'
Whose heart has ne'er within him burned..."

Try as she might, Sara could not put excitement into that poem, even though she was famed for her dramatic recitations. For the sake of Hetty, Miss Stacey tried hard to muster some enthusiasm, even though she, too, saw at once that the poem was less than a crowd-pleaser.

"It's not a very interesting poem, is it?" Sara ventured after she had finished.

"Well," said Miss Stacey, treading very carefully on Hetty's ground, "it *is* Sir Walter Scott, but I do know that he isn't everybody's cup of tea, as they say."

She thought hard for a moment, then brightened.

"Class...I think I have just had a rather good idea."

Miss Stacey thought the idea so good that she hopped down from the wagon again and began to pace a little bit with newfound elation. The next thing the children knew, Miss Stacey had taken a seat on the boards right in the midst of them as they hurriedly shifted to make room.

"Don't you think," Miss Stacey said in a breathless voice, "that the Lieutenant Governor's reception might be the perfect occasion...to have a little tribute to Miss King?"

Felix blinked at Miss Stacey as though she had gone crazy.

"For Aunt Hetty? What the heck for?"

"Because she deserves it, of course," Miss Stacey replied staunchly. "I don't know how much all of you happen to be aware of this, but Miss King is one of the most respected teachers on Prince Edward Island."

"I think it's a wonderful idea, Miss Stacey," Sara Stanley chimed in, seeing a golden chance to cheer up her Aunt Hetty and escape the boring poem. "Could we do it with music, too?"

"Oh yes, and dancing!" Miss Stacey added extravagantly, her eyes lighting up with an imagination very much like Sara's. "But we must keep it a secret. We want this to be a complete surprise for Miss King. Now, do I have your solemn promise?"

Each head nodded as all the children willingly joined the conspiracy. Miss Stacey clapped her hands together, looking positively girlish, for there was nothing she loved better than cooking up a good mystery.

"Not a word to anyone," she warned with a wink. "All right? Now that we're all agreed, let's gather round and put our heads together."

Another first! The children were actually being consulted in the planning. They hopped off the boards and gathered in a circle around Miss Stacey, each one suddenly bubbling over with ideas for the show.

Chapter Ten

Back at Rose Cottage, Hetty was suffering not only the pains in her back but the attentions of three female visitors, all of them agog with curiosity about what had actually befallen the invalid. Luckily, the true story about the ignominious tumble into the bathtub remained a secret, sealed up forever in the bosoms of those involved. Sara and Olivia knew it was as much as their lives were worth to repeat it. And Miss Stacey, so far, seemed uninterested in using the information to her own advantage. Nevertheless, Mrs. Potts, Mrs. Spencer and Mrs. Biggins all eyed Hetty avidly, on the hunt, Hetty didn't doubt, for a succulent piece of gossip to carry back to Avonlea.

Hetty was not in the best of positions to repel invaders. She sat propped up by pillows and hot-water bottles on the parlor sofa, feeling very much like a cornered badger. Her visitors ranged themselves in a semicircle, drinking tea and surreptitiously examining Hetty for signs of her mishap. Olivia, on whom now fell all the duties of hostess, bustled up with an array of luscious chocolates all arranged on one of Rose Cottage's best china plates. Hetty loved chocolates, and Olivia had put them out hoping her sister might take some comfort from the rich confections.

"Some chocolate, Hetty? Miss Stacey sent them."

Hetty, whose fingers had actually been extended, snatched her hand back. Despite her partiality for chocolate, especially such fine ones as lay temptingly on the plate, she muttered and waved Olivia brusquely away.

"No."

Distressed, Olivia turned to the guests.

"Mrs. Biggins?"

Mrs. Biggins helped herself to a fat one filled with almond cream. As Olivia moved on to Mrs. Potts, Mrs. Potts was looking Hetty up and down.

"Hetty King, you're looking rather green around the gills. Perhaps you should try a tonic." She paused only to grab a whole handful of chocolates, much to Olivia's quiet disgust. "Muriel Stacey recommends tonic very highly."

Mrs. Potts knew very well how much that name would irritate Hetty, and she said it just to see its effect. Hetty tossed her head. If Muriel Stacey recommended tonics, Hetty meant to have nothing to do with them.

"Wouldn't touch them," she sniffed. "Tonics are for weak-livered souls." Her look implied that perhaps Muriel Stacey's liver was not in the best of conditions.

Mrs. Spencer exchanged a glance with Mrs. Potts and refused to let up on the subject that grated on Hetty so gratifyingly.

"Wasn't Muriel Stacey's talk last night at the Biggins's just marvelous?" Mrs. Spencer sighed with an air of innocence. "I had no idea the arts were all the rage!"

Oh, so besides taking over people's schools, Muriel Stacey was now giving lectures at the boarding house, too. Despite her efforts to seem unaffected, Hetty looked about ready to start grinding her teeth on the edge of the parlor table. Mrs. Potts, having her victim helpless before her, was not about to let the opportunity pass without wringing the greatest amount of satisfaction possible from it. She picked up the newspaper from the side table.

"Oh, Hetty, here's Olivia's article," she chirped, exactly as though she had just stumbled across it by accident and hadn't known it was there all along.

"Ladies!" She held up one fat hand and began to read aloud. "'Avonlea's two favorite teachers: things you didn't know. By Olivia King.'"

This time Hetty couldn't hide how much she was startled, even though the paper had been lying within reach all morning. It was true that Olivia had had a job of sorts with the Avonlea *Chronicle* for some time now, searching out local news, reporting on tea parties and such like. Hetty regarded the job as just a bit of silliness on Olivia's part, when Olivia might better spend her time making herself useful around Rose Cottage, where she belonged. The last thing Hetty ever expected to see was Olivia's name on an article about a member of her own family.

Stiffly, Hetty sat through the "oohs" and "aahs" as Mrs. Potts read the printed column. Eventually, the "oohs" changed to smothered snickers, then broke into outright laughter. Olivia, who had just finished pouring everyone a cool drink, hovered near the doorway, growing more and more dismayed at how her article was being treated.

"'Differences are the spice of life,'" Mrs. Potts recited, mincing each word a little for effect. "'Miss Muriel Stacey, who is staying for a brief time in Avonlea, and Miss Hetty King are modern career women who have remarkably differing tastes. For example: for breakfast, Miss Stacey adores strawberries and muffins with apple butter and coffee. Miss King prefers porridge, no salt.'"

"No salt!" rasped Mrs. Spencer to Hetty, making a face. "Must taste like horse feed."

"'For her beauty routine,'" Mrs Potts continued, "'Miss Stacey is fond of English powder and French night cream.'"

"Sounds expensive!" Mrs. Spencer cooed in awe.

"'Miss King sticks to soap and water.'"

Hetty was done putting a good face on things. Rather than be subjected to any more, she made a mighty effort to get up, fully intending to stomp from the room. She forgot about her strained back muscles; she was doubled over in pain the next moment and collapsed back among the tumbled sofa cushions.

Mrs. Spencer sprang solicitously to her aid.

"Oooh, Hetty, let me help you up, dear."

"No, I'm fine," Hetty growled, bent only on escape. "I'm fine. Just need a little exercise, that's all. I'm stiff, you see. Carry on."

"Stiff," drawled Mrs. Biggins, nodding her head knowingly to the others.

"Stiff," Mrs. Potts repeated, shutting her lips in a little smirk.

"*Stiff*," confirmed Hetty defiantly, heaving herself to her feet at last in spite of it all. Shaking off Mrs. Spencer and fiercely stifling her grimaces of pain, Hetty grabbed the cane leaning against the sofa arm and hobbled towards the kitchen, supporting herself on one piece of furniture after the other as she went. The furious glare she shot at Olivia left her sister in no doubt as to Hetty's feelings. When the parlor door swung shut behind Hetty, the other women rocked forward in their chairs, tittering.

"Well, soap's cheap and water's free," whispered Mrs. Potts, poking fun at Hetty's beauty routine.

Mrs. Potts took up the newspaper again. Her audience was spellbound, and the information Olivia had provided was just too fascinating to miss.

"'Their favorite books: Miss Stacey loves *Pride and Prejudice*. Miss King recommends the Bible. Their favorite vacation: last spring, Miss Stacey enjoyed a barge cruise on the River Seine. Miss King took the ferry to Halifax.'"

Ferry to Halifax! This last was just too much. Abandoning their last efforts to politely restrain themselves, all three of the women burst into riotous shrieks of laughter.

Hetty managed to reach the refuge of the kitchen and lower herself, groaning, into a chair. No sooner had she sat herself down than she all but jumped up again, for the hilarity of the visitors in the parlor carried all the way down the hall and struck Hetty like a bucket of cold water. Then Olivia came rushing in after her, carrying a half-empty pitcher in her hand.

"Hetty..." she breathed distractedly, trying to think of something to say about the fiasco in the parlor.

Hetty turned a white-lipped glare on Olivia. She was clutching the corner of the kitchen table to hold herself upright and looked as though she would have sprung at Olivia like an scalded wildcat had her injured back only permitted.

"Olivia King, I could wring your neck!"

More peals of mirth punctuated the scene in the kitchen. Olivia dropped weakly into a chair.

"I'm sorry. I thought it would make you sound sensible."

"Hah! Sensible!" Hetty flung back, telltale spots of fury appearing on her cheeks. "About as sensible as an old dish rag. They're not laughing at Muriel Stacey, you nincompoop, they're laughing at me!"

Olivia had never been safe from Hetty's outrage. The words of the article flashed again through Olivia's mind, this time as Hetty must have heard them. Why, oh, why hadn't she realized how dreadful all those nice sensible things would sound when compared to the fascinating life of Muriel Stacey! Now she had wounded Hetty and made her a laughingstock to boot. It was all too much for

Olivia. Her lip began to quiver and her hands to shake, splashing the juice remaining in the pitcher. Without so much as a sniffle of warning, Olivia plopped the pitcher down and burst loudly into tears.

Chapter Eleven

Miss Stacey was very serious indeed about making an impression at the Lieutenant Governor's reception. She set about planning the children's performance with the crack efficiency that had made her the success she was. Not only that, she actually paid attention to the suggestions of the children, making the performance a cooperative effort on everyone's part. Acting on Sara Stanley's enthusiastic idea about including music, Miss Stacey had organized a musicale, and she worked hard at helping the children learn their roles.

However, even Miss Stacey couldn't get everything perfect. In her efforts to include everyone, one of her ideas was to have Sara and Felix sing a duet. Sara had a sweet, clear voice, but Felix, poor fellow, didn't have a scrap of musical ability in him. The whole school, including Gus, who sat chewing his pencil, listened with some discomfort to Sara and Felix running through their number at the front of the room. Sara had very elevated ideas about what a song for the Lieutenant Governor should sound like. She winced in frustration as Felix rasped and croaked beside her, so off-key that even the window panes seemed to rattle.

"...and listen to me,
I'll sing you a song of the fish of the sea,
It's windy weather, for stormy weather,
But when the wind blows, we're all together,
Blow, you winds westerly,
Blow, you winds, blow..."

They had just got to "jolly sou-westerly" when Sara was finally driven to clap her hands over her ears.

"...steady, she goes!" Felix belted out, squawking like two rusty scythe blades scraped together.

"Children!" Miss Stacey snapped in spite of herself. Even as teacher, she could no longer remain impartial about Felix's abysmal lack of talent.

"Miss Stacey, Felix is singing out of tune on purpose," Sara accused, unable to believe that anyone could be that bad just naturally.

"I am not," Felix fired back. "And besides, what makes you so perfect?"

Sara's chin thrust out dangerously, for she was practically certain Felix was out to spoil their beautiful duet just so he could get out of singing it. Felix, equally sure he was being unjustly incriminated, began to glower at his cousin.

Recognizing all the danger signals, Felicity leaped in to save the situation before a genuine scrap could break out. Felicity adored having Miss Stacey in the classroom, adored the plan for the musicale and meant to prevent anything from upsetting it if she could. She also knew a few things about the pupils in the school that Miss Stacey did not.

"Miss Stacey, Felix has no talent at all. He should paint scenery. Gus is the most talented musician in the class. He could play his fiddle and accompany Sara. It's right there in the cupboard."

Of course, Felicity omitted telling Miss Stacey just why the fiddle was in the cupboard in the first place. A sudden dead silence fell on the room, puzzling the teacher as she crossed to the cupboard, opened the door and saw the instrument, which had dust on it, probably for the first time in many years. The sight of its curving sides made her face light up. Why, they might be able to have real music with their musicale!

"What an excellent idea, Felicity," Miss Stacey cried, lifting the fiddle out. "Isn't this wonderful. Is this yours, Gus? How marvelous! I didn't know you could play. Please, give us a tune."

In a gesture Hetty King would never have countenanced in her classroom, Miss Stacey held the fiddle out to Gus. For a moment, Gus forgot everything but his intense longing to play. His gaze devoured the familiar instrument hungrily. Then, Hetty's dire words ringing in his ears, he stiffened and turned away, a kind of panic in his eyes.

"I don't play no more," he answered hoarsely.

In the electric silence, Miss Stacey stepped closer with the fiddle. She loved music quite as much as Felicity and imagined vividly how some real fiddle playing would improve the musicale.

"Gus, fiddle music would make such an exciting contribution to the tribute for Miss King. All the other children are taking part. Isn't there anything we can do to convince you to join us?"

Muriel Stacey at her most persuasive was a hard woman to refuse, but refuse her Gus did. Steadfastly looking away from the instrument that was once almost a physical part of him, Gus shook his head.

"Are you sure?" Miss Stacey asked, growing more and more perplexed by Gus's behavior. Why did the boy own a fiddle if he didn't want to play?

"Got these words to copy out, Miss Stacey," Gus mumbled, dropping his head and going doggedly, pointedly, back to working on his slate.

As Gus labored over his letters, ignoring Miss Stacey, the teacher paused, torn between trying a further appeal and leaving the matter alone. Something in Gus's expression made her sigh softly, return to her desk and slip the fiddle back onto the cupboard shelf. As she did, she couldn't miss the disappointment of the other children, too, at this stubborn self-denial on the part of music-loving Gus.

Despite her apparent compliance on that occasion, Miss Stacey was not one to give up on a project. She had read all the pained longing in the lad's face when she had first offered him the fiddle. She knew she needed to talk to Gus, and talk to him without the presence of a school full of listening little ears. So she waited patiently until late that afternoon, sometime after school had been dismissed, and then made her way to the cannery.

She looked just as out of place walking along the dock as had Hetty King, except that Miss Stacey was a good deal less offended by the smell and a good deal more curious about everything she saw. She made her way carefully along the worn wood, looking this way and that.

"Please," she inquired of the first worker she came to, "where can I find Gus Pike?"

The man, a gnarled old character who was beginning to wonder why the cannery attracted so many schoolteachers, nodded his head towards one of the sheds.

"He's round the corner, Ma'am."

"Thank you." Miss Stacey smiled and headed in the direction the man had pointed out. There she did find Gus, at work, sorting fish into different barrels. He was working hard, with the same concentration he applied to his school notebook, his hands quick and agile at the smelly, slippery job.

"Do you help to catch the fish, as well?" she asked from just behind him.

Gus jumped at the familiar voice, almost losing a big cod over the side of the dock into the water. When he swung round and saw Miss Stacey standing there, he did his best to make a quick recovery from his surprise.

"Oh, some, if they're short a man," he told her, flipping another fish to the side. "I fill the tubs for the baited trawl. You ask me, handlines work better."

At this sage opinion in one so young, Miss Stacey smiled and stepped closer under the lacy parasol she carried.

"You seem to know a great deal about cannery work, Gus. Yet Felicity tells me that you've only been at this a couple of months this summer."

My, my, schoolteachers were corkers at finding out about a guy! This Miss Stacey hadn't even been in Avonlea for a week and already she knew what Gus worked at and for how long. Her praise and her interest made Gus flush with pleasure. He gulped and kept on talking.

"There's plenty to learn 'bout fish—'bout anything—if ya got the hunger."

"The hunger?"

"Yeah."

Gus almost left it at that, but Miss Stacey's eyes were fixed on him, kind and intrigued. He had never revealed this much of himself to anyone before, but there was something about Miss Stacey that just drew confidences out of a fellow.

"I got all these questions," he confessed.

"Ah, what sort of questions would they be?" Miss Stacey inquired. Her eyes were lighting up with the same spark of fascination that Hetty's had when she'd first discovered Gus.

Gus shrugged, as though puzzled by his own inner workings, the things that made him different from the other fellows in the bunkhouse, who were content just to work and eat and sleep and poke fun at anyone who did otherwise.

"Don't know. At night, I think about things. It gets dark, I hear the quiet...I start thinkin'."

"About why you don't play the fiddle anymore?" Miss Stacey asked quietly, grasping the chance to find out what she had really come to discover.

Sore trouble flooded into Gus's face, and he dropped his head.

"Miss King...tol' me stuff...how I'd wreck my life."

Dumbfounded, Miss Stacey stared at Gus. She would never have supposed that Gus had such drastic ideas in his head.

"Wreck your life? But why on earth would Miss King say anything like that?"

Gus could barely look at Miss Stacey because of the fear in his eyes. Up until now, he had had no one to really teach him anything. In spite of his intelligence, he was prey to all sorts of superstitions. Hetty King's words had merely brought all the accumulated fears together and focused them on himself.

"It's my father's fiddle. He kilt a fella. I think it's cursed."

Cursed! This was far worse than even Miss Stacy could have imagined. She now had to do something to repair the damage Hetty had inadvertently caused.

"That's why you're so afraid," she told him softly. "But Gus, it just isn't so."

All the muscles in Gus's young face tightened and he shook his head. Hetty King was now his idol, all-seeing and all-knowing. If she said a thing, then it surely must be so.

"Nope. She can see inside me. Miss King saw the angel, an' she saw the devil, the two of them, fightin' away."

The idea of Hetty King wielding such supernatural powers would have been hilarious had Gus not taken her words so seriously. His torment was so plain it broke Miss Stacey's heart. Only just barely did she prevent herself from trying to comfort him with a touch of her hand. Instead, she took a firmer grip on her parasol.

"Do I have your permission to talk with Miss King about what you've just told me?"

It was obvious that the only person who could change Gus's mind was Hetty herself, but Gus shook his head, discouraged.

"Ain't no use. She ain't gonna hear ya. An' ya know why? 'Cause she's right."

Gus began furiously sorting fish again, mostly to cover the fact that his lower lip was quivering and his eyes, big lad though he was, were threatening to spill out tears. Miss Stacey could see that he was utterly miserable. She also saw that it would be useless to speak to him further on the matter. She paused a long moment, then turned and marched off down the dock again, leaving Gus to his work and his dejected thoughts.

Determined to repair matters, Miss Stacey went straight to Rose Cottage, where she and Hetty, thanks to Olivia, were soon set up in the parlor in front of cake and tea. Stuck at home, Hetty had had considerable time to stew over the dreadful things Muriel Stacey was probably perpetrating in her classroom. A palpable tension crackled in the room between the two women.

"Hetty," Miss Stacey began firmly, "I might as well be blunt. I've come about Gus Pike."

"Gus? What's he done now?"

Hetty took a sip from her teacup and regarded her visitor piercingly over the rim. If Gus Pike were causing trouble, she seemed to say, it was most likely because Muriel Stacey didn't know the proper way to teach.

"That's just it. He hasn't done anything, yet I've never seen a boy more unhappy," Miss Stacey said, unflinching in Hetty's gaze.

Hetty almost choked on a mouthful of tea.

"Unhappy? What do you mean? He's in school, he's learning to read and write. What's he got to be unhappy about?"

Ever the teacher, sometimes Hetty couldn't see beyond the student to the whole person. Miss Stacey set down her cup and took a breath.

"Hetty, Gus holds you in higher regard than anyone else on this earth, yet he misses his fiddle terribly. You've made him afraid even to touch it."

Hetty's cup rattled on its saucer as Hetty looked her guest up and down and bristled.

"That's what you're up to, is it? I should have known," she rapped out. "I'll not have you undermining my rules! I've told him, no fiddle."

It hadn't taken Miss Stacey long to come up

against the steel in Hetty's personality. Making an effort to remain calm, she lowered her voice.

"Hetty...I'm begging you, just this once, bend."

She might as well have suggested that Hetty dance a jig in front of the general store. Hetty's head flew up.

"Bend! I can't bend. The children wouldn't respect me."

"Hetty, sometimes you can talk such nonsense!" cried Miss Stacey, exasperation at last getting the better of her. "I can't understand—"

"I understand all right," Hetty shot back, her eyes flashing as though she knew every dastardly plot Muriel Stacey had been up to. "You'd do anything to get those children on your side, wouldn't you?"

"Hetty, really!"

"Gus Pike has bad habits. It's in his nature."

Shocked by Hetty's obstinance, Miss Stacey rose to her feet, indignation flushing her face under the fine English powder. There seemed no point in continuing the argument.

"Well, I'm sorry you feel that way...truly sorry."

Having barely touched her tea, Miss Stacey turned grandly and swept out, leaving Hetty propped on the sofa, clutching a piece of pound cake in one hand and looking distinctly more uncomfortable than Hetty King generally liked to feel.

Chapter Twelve

After Miss Stacey left the cannery, Gus threw himself into his job, sweating and laboring in a vain attempt to work off the feverish tumble of emotion built up inside him. Without his music as an outlet for his feelings, he felt as if a great swelling was building up in his chest, getting bigger every day. He did his best to pay no mind to it, for he was determined to learn to read and write. He was also determined to escape the clutches of the devil that had got hold of his father and would surely get him if he gave in to the lure of music and dancing. Miss King was the schoolteacher and she knew what to do. He would follow her orders, even if it meant he had to explode right there on the dock where he stood.

Sticking to his resolve proved far harder than Gus had bargained for, especially when his co-workers were always pestering him to give them a tune. That evening proved no different. After the crew had knocked off after a day of hard, repetitive work, they, quite naturally, felt they had earned some entertainment.

As always, the first thing they did was build themselves a bonfire beside the cannery to ward off the night chill. In its leaping yellow light, they gave themselves up to laughing and carousing and doing their best to have a good time. Since Gus had given up music, they had had to recruit an older man to play the fiddle for their rollicking dances. The man wasn't half as good as Gus had been, for his bow sawed and squawked, torturing the poor fiddle along with the listeners' ears. Only the amount of drink consumed and the loudness of the yells interspersed with the music lent the playing a semblance of a tune at all.

Gus hovered about the fire, too, but he neither drank nor danced. He didn't even talk to anybody. In fact, he stood about with his hands jammed into his pockets, feeling about as wretched as a fellow could feel who no longer seemed to fit in here with his mates nor anywhere else that he could think of. With a longing he wasn't even aware of, Gus watched the other fiddler stomping his foot and nodding his head vigorously to keep time. Lost, Gus stood unaware of Pincher until Pincher was right at his shoulder. Pincher had had too much to drink already and was in an aggressive mood. He didn't like the way Gus had been spending all his spare time scribbling in his notebook and holding himself apart from the general run of things. Education, Pincher decided, was making Gus too big for his britches.

"Hey, schoolboy!" he taunted. "Teacher wipe the

snot off yer nose? What's the matter? You too smart for us now?"

Gus paid Pincher no attention at all, which only riled Pincher further. Like many a fellow used to wallowing in the mire, Pincher felt personally affronted when anyone else tried to climb out of it.

"Hey, I'm talkin' to ya," Pincher yelled over the din. And for good measure he gave Gus a kick to get his attention. "Hey, chicken! Forgot how to fight?"

Pincher might have thought it safe to kick Gus, since Gus was usually such a peaceable fellow. Pincher had no conception of the pressure building up in Gus, pressure that needed to be let out. The kick caught Gus exactly in the mood for a fight, and Gus hadn't forgotten how, for no lad can hang about docks and trawlers and fish canneries without having to defend himself once in a while. Full to the brim as he was with worked-up feelings, Gus could be forgiven for taking them out on the nearest convenient object—which happened to be Pincher.

Since Pincher had proved so provoking, Gus suddenly sprang round, hauled off and smashed him a good one in the side of the jaw. Pincher went reeling backwards so hard he slammed into the shed wall and made it shake. For an instant, he blinked at Gus in stunned surprise. Then, shaking his head like a bull trying to clear off bees, he righted himself, let out a bellow and charged at Gus with all his might.

"Fight! Fight!" shouted the rest of the workers, promptly dropping whatever they were doing to watch the spectacle. Gleefully, they gathered around in a circle as the two boys writhed and wrestled on the dusty ground. This was exactly the sort of rough sport the cannery workers loved. They began to cheer and yell and pick one or the other of the combatants as their favorite to win.

The fight was soon in panting earnest, with the two boys rolling and stumbling and trying to get a telling hold on some vital body part. Gus took swings at Pincher and Pincher took swings back. Pincher managed to bloody Gus's nose even as Gus sent Pincher's hat flying and grabbed a great handful of Pincher's hair, fully intending to pull it out by the roots if he could. Dust rose in a cloud from their struggles and yelling spectators had to jump out of the way as the two boys rolled about in the circle.

The battle provided such a distraction that no one paid the least attention to the shed where Pincher's thump against a wall had jarred a high shelf. On that shelf, a can of kerosene fell over, unnoticed by everyone, and began trickling its contents down the dry, weathered walls of the shed towards the ground. Even this accident might not have been so terrible if the flying heels of the boys had not struck a corner, this time jarring loose a lantern from its nail. The lantern fell upside down into a pile of old, bleached fishing nets heaped against the shed. There the lantern smoked, its tiny flame trying to make up its mind whether or not it would go out.

Just when Gus had twisted, eel-like, and got Pincher down underneath him, he felt himself lifted up by his collar and roughly jerked aside. Angus McCorkadale had come out of the cannery office, where he had been at work, and waded furiously into the fray.

"Break it up! Break it up!" he bellowed. "Get 'em apart!"

With the appearance of the boss, a dozen hands were suddenly helping to drag the two lads away from each other. Angus McCorkadale, much put out with such rowdiness, shook his fist at Gus.

"I warned you, Pike!"

No one bothered to inform Angus that it was really Pincher who had started the fight. Forcibly parted from the struggle, Gus stood where he had been pushed, breathing heavily, his dander up and the fire of battle shooting through his veins. With the fight stopped, he needed another outlet for his feelings and needed it fast.

Defiantly, he eyed the stubble-faced man who was still playing the fiddle, and had played it all through the scuffle. In a single stride, Gus had snatched the fiddle clean out of the fellow's hands and jammed it under his chin. The next moment, he started to play, and play more wildly than he had ever played in his life before. His foot stomped, and the mad reel flew up at the stars as Gus made it into a vent for his seething inner storm of emotion. A shiver shot through the crowd at the intensity of the whirling notes and the taut expression on Gus's face. They would have all begun to dance, as though compelled, had not the tiny flame in the tumbled lantern decided on life, crawled into the dry fishing nets and then found the trickling kerosene.

Eerily, as though conjured by the music itself, the flicker became a blaze and the blaze shot up the side of the shed to the kerosene can, where it suddenly exploded towards the sky, leaving the wall nothing but a soaring sheet of flame.

"Hey, look there! Fire!"

People stared for one fascinated second, then began shouting and waving their arms and bumping into one another in their efforts to do something fast. Everything was in an uproar. Angus McCorkadale, his whole cannery only a stone's throw from the shed, leaped round as though on fire himself.

"Water!" he roared. "Get some water!"

Everyone started running madly to the rescue, except Gus. Gus stood frozen to the spot, gaping at the swirling orange inferno gobbling at the shingles of the shed roof. Slowly, very slowly, he took the fiddle out from under his chin. Slowly, but with utter horror, he looked from the fire to the fiddle and back again. Hetty King was right. His music was cursed! Against Hetty's orders he had given in to the temptation, and a devil had sent the fire as punishment.

Luckily for the cannery, there was a whole sea full of water available just under the dock. The men, despite everything they had had to drink, set up fire lines and slung the water frantically at the flames. They managed to act swiftly enough so that the fire didn't spread.

If the damages had only stopped there, matters might have been quite reparable. However, what was destroyed that night, along with the wooden shed, was Gus's belief in himself. He spent a night racked with guilt and spiritual torment. When he came to school the next day, it was only to announce that he was quitting.

The news was distressing in the extreme to Miss Stacey, who stood at the front of the classroom, her brows pulled into a frustrated frown. The rest of the children sat motionless in their seats, all eyes and ears as Gus shifted in humiliation in front of his teacher. Miss Stacey was opening the cupboard and taking out Gus's fiddle.

"We all understand how badly you feel, Gus," she told him sympathetically, "but you mustn't blame yourself. The fire was an accident. Please don't quit school."

Gus only looked more stubborn, with smudges under his eyes from smoke and the long, sleepless night he had spent. He had his own code of honor. If he'd been the cause of the shed burning down, he now had to do his utmost to put things right.

"I'm goin' back to work full time. Gonna pay off the damages to Mr. McCorkadale."

Apparently, Angus McCorkadale hadn't been backward about pinning the blame on Gus either— a pretty easy thing to do when Gus already blamed himself.

Miss Stacey fingered the fiddle she was holding. In her hands, it looked innocent and cheerful, certainly not like the devil's tool, reeking of sulphur and brimstone, as Gus now thought it was.

"Please reconsider. You have so much ability."

Gus shook his head despairingly. His mind was made up about himself and just might remain that way for the rest of his life.

"Ain't no sense in it. I got bad blood in me. I ain't comin' back. I'll take my fiddle, Miss Stacey."

Even as Gus held out his hand, the door at the back flew open and Hetty King burst into the room. She was bent over painfully and hobbling with a cane, but hobbling fast nevertheless. She was just in time to see Miss Stacey hand the fiddle over to Gus.

"Muriel Stacey!" Hetty sputtered. "How could you give that fiddle to the boy when I asked you not to?"

Gus stared in consternation at Hetty, snatched the fiddle and bolted out the side door as though ten demons were after him.

"Gus Pike, come back here," Hetty shouted after him. How dare one of her pupils decamp without permission?

"Hetty!" Miss Stacey admonished before pulling open the door Gus had fled through. "Gus!" she called out, but it was no use. Gus was gone, and Hetty was bearing down on her.

"Just what do you mean by—"

Hetty halted, suddenly aware of all the staring children, children who would all carry home colorful accounts of what happened today in the classroom. She made an awkward turn on her cane towards the door.

"Little pitchers have big ears. I'd like a word with you in private, Miss Stacey."

Miss Stacey didn't need to be asked twice. Both teachers stepped outside. Hetty carefully closed the school door behind her and faced her counterpart in a fury, unaware that all the children had rushed to the window, the better to stare down at the scene.

"First, behind my back, it seems, you've undone years of my hard work, turned my classroom into a carnival, and now this—the fiddle!"

"Oh, Hetty, that's not the way it is at all," Miss Stacey explained in exasperation. "Not a bit of it. I didn't give Gus Pike back his fiddle. He took it back, because he just quit school."

"He what?" cried Hetty, completely taken aback.

"It seems there was a bit of a to-do at the cannery last night. The boys at the bunkhouse got to fighting, and somehow a fire broke out, and the shed burned down."

Fire was always a very serious matter in a countryside full of wooden buildings. Hetty frowned in worry.

"Oh, good grief. Was anyone hurt?"

"No, thankfully. But Angus McCorkadale blames Gus, so Gus has quit school in order to pay off the damages to McCorkadale."

"Quit school! Oh, he can't quit school. It's his only chance to…"

Muriel Stacey was generally a kindly, tolerant person, but even she had her limits. She drew her mouth tight and squared her shoulders. It was time to drop some home truths on Hetty King.

"Hetty, I am loath to tell you this, truly I am, but I

must. If Gus Pike has quit school, it's because of you."

Completely forgetting the stabbing pains in her back, Hetty reared up in offended pique.

"Me?" she spat. "What are you saying, woman?"

Miss Stacey took a couple of troubled steps in the cool morning grass, still much put out with Hetty.

"Don't you see how much he loves his music? He's perfectly miserable without it. Yet because of something that you said, he's taken this terrible notion that his fiddle is something cursed. And after the fire last night, he's even more convinced of it than ever."

Even Hetty was capable of getting the point after a while. As Miss Stacey's meaning finally sank in, Hetty's hand flew to her mouth in distress.

"Good Lord, Muriel. I never meant anything that far-fetched."

"Hetty, he'll listen to you. Talk to him."

This time the plea reached Hetty in its entirety and its urgency. Hetty could be just as forceful as Muriel Stacey once she made up her mind. Now, she realized she had better take action immediately or Gus would be lost to education forever.

As Muriel Stacey went back into the school, Hetty hobbled back to Rose Cottage, got the buggy and headed straight for the cannery, gritting her teeth over every bump as the buggy-springs jarred the sore muscles of her back.

Once there, she climbed stiffly down and hobbled slowly along the dock, looking this way and that among the workers until she finally spotted Gus. He was stacking dried fish and didn't see her until she called out his name.

"Gus Pike!"

Gus whirled around.

"Miss King!"

Painfully, Hetty limped over to him, unmindful that Gus was as astonished to see her as if a ghost had risen up from the ground. She was suffering stabs along her spine and had a big pill to swallow in the form of a confession. Hetty King was not very used to confessions.

"It's taken a lot for me to come here," she announced briskly, "so I want you to listen and listen hard."

Gus wiped his hands on his jacket and avoided her eyes.

"I'd like to say I've been wrong," Hetty went on, saying words few in Avonlea had ever been privileged to hear from her. "I'm not accustomed to it; however, I do believe I did do something wrong where you're concerned."

Miss King admitting she was wrong! Gus would hardly hear of it. He opened his mouth to object, but Hetty overrode him.

"No, not a word out of you, boy. You ruin the King's English, so you may as well let me do the talking. Now, when I spoke to you about that fiddle, I never meant you'd end up in prison like your father! I only meant that the fiddle stopped you concentrating in school."

"But you saw the devil in me. You did," Gus protested, still fervently believing in Hetty's powers of clairvoyance and thought-reading.

"Well, there's some devil in most people. Not in me, mind you," Hetty amended hastily, removing herself from the bulk of the human race, "but in most. Yes, you've got your share..."

Seeing the expression on Gus's face, she stopped, for she was getting on tricky ground again. No need to plant any more doubts in him than he already had.

"But you've also got a mind that, properly nurtured, could lead you to great heights," she told him emphatically, leaping straight to the positive. "You should think hard about coming back to school, Gus. I believe," and here Hetty couldn't prevent her voice from cracking a little, "I'd miss you if you didn't."

Not trusting herself to say more, Hetty pivoted about and limped off down the dock again. Gus stood looking after her, his face full of confusion, longing and a wondrous, dawning surprise that anyone as impressive as Hetty King could miss a cannery boy like him.

Chapter Thirteen

Almost before the schoolchildren of Avonlea knew it, the day of the Lieutenant Governor's reception had arrived. The event was to be held at the White Sands Hotel, the grandest establishment in the neighborhood and the only fit setting in which to hold such a magnificent affair. The White Sands Hotel was a large, gabled fantasy of a building set amidst rolling green lawns that swept down to the sea. At the edge of the lawns lay the sparkling white beaches from which the hotel took its name. Wealthy people came from all over the continent to holiday there, breathe in the bracing sea air and enjoy all the luxuries offered in the hotel's elegant interior.

The reception was heralded by brightly polished buggies driving up the broad, graveled driveway and by elegantly dressed people strolling across the manicured lawns towards the hotel. Inside, flags, flowers and great crystal bowls brimming with punch proclaimed the reception a truly gala event. Ladies and gentlemen strolled about, showing off their new finery. All the new hats ordered at Lawson's store were now working for their keep, including the one with the bows perched firmly on Hetty King's head.

The ballroom of the White Sands had been filled with chairs, and those chairs were soon filled with a jam-packed audience that crowded itself into the room for the formal presentations. Hetty was seated at the front with Olivia watching the event she was most interested in: the performance of the children from the Avonlea school. Because of her injury, she had been unable to get back into the classroom in the time leading up to the reception. Now, she could only pray that Muriel Stacey hadn't ruined the presentation Hetty had been working so hard on before her fall.

Dressed in ribbons and bows and painstakingly pressed new suits, the children were ranged across the stage, just finishing the poem they had practiced under Hetty's tutelage. Following Sara's lead, they were doing their best to try to inject some spirit into it. The audience, which included the parents of most of the children, was giving its full attention, Hetty noted. Certainly the Lieutenant Governor and his wife, seated front and center, appeared to be watching with interest. Hetty nodded approvingly as the children swept towards what she thought of as the very satisfying conclusion of the work.

"Despite these titles, power and pelf,
The wretch concerned all in self
Living shall forfeit fair renown,

And doubly dying, shall go down
To the vile dust from whence he sprung,
Unwept, unhonored and unsung."

With vast and not very secret relief, the children finished the monotonous verse and bowed. A moment of rather soporific quiet followed before the audience, which had not, perhaps, been paying as much heed as Hetty believed, suddenly realized the recitation was over. Hurriedly, it produced a scatter of polite applause which Hetty acknowledged by bowing primly to the right and to the left.

"See," Hetty said to Olivia, ignoring the scanty enthusiasm the work had roused among its listeners. "I knew they'd love the poem."

Olivia cast a skeptical glance at her sister and had sense enough to keep her comments to herself. A good thing, too, for the people suddenly burst into real applause, loud and enthusiastic, when Muriel Stacey glided out before them. As Miss Stacey lifted her hand for attention, Hetty's brows flew together stormily: she was certain the woman was bent on stealing all the credit for herself.

"Thank you, children. Thank you," Miss Stacey trilled charmingly. "And now, Your Excellency, Mrs. Vaughn." She nodded towards the appropriate dignitaries. "With your kind permission, I would like to request that the assembly please remain seated.

The pupils of Avonlea school have prepared a special tribute to someone whom they greatly respect and admire."

Hetty all but gave a scandalized gasp aloud. Trust Muriel Stacey to take advantage of her grip on the Avonlea school to cook up yet one more way to show off.

"Someone," Miss Stacey continued, looking significantly over to where Hetty sat and smiling even wider, "who has given unselfishly for so long, not only to this school, but to the entire community—Miss Hetty King!"

As everyone twisted to look, Hetty was caught with the scowl still on her face and her mouth in the act of dropping open in astonishment. Her hand darted to her bosom as if to contain the great thumps her heart was suddenly taking. Her mouth flew shut again. Acute embarrassment fought hard with the happy smile that simply welled up on her face as the meaning of Muriel Stacey's words gradually sank in. Even the Lieutenant Governor himself turned in his seat to acknowledge her. It was just as though she were really the honored guest she had dreamed of being the day the letter from the Board of Education arrived. The audience again burst into applause—heartfelt applause this time—and Miss Stacey gestured to the youngsters on stage.

"Quickly, children," she whispered under her breath, "time to get ready for our tribute."

Anxious to keep events rolling, Miss Stacey hustled the children off to the side so that they could prepare. Just as she was about to turn away, she stopped mid-step and stood motionless, staring over the heads of the crowd. Naturally, the audience turned around in their seats to look too. There, in the ornate entranceway to the ballroom, a slim, young figure hesitated, trying to get up the courage to come in.

The newcomer was none other than Gus Pike. Amazingly, Gus was scrubbed clean from top to toe, even to his ears and his fingernails. Not only that, he had from somewhere commandeered shoes, respectable trousers, a clean white shirt, a fresh collar and a carefully knotted tie—evidence that he must have been pouring over Hetty's book for days.

Even more incredible, he was clutching his old fiddle lovingly under his arm, just as though he had never once been parted from it. His face was pale but very determined, as though he were swallowing down a good deal of fright.

"Gus!" Miss Stacey exclaimed.

"Gus Pike!" Hetty repeated in a whisper to Olivia. "What's he doing here?"

It seemed they were soon going to find out. Gus stepped through the door and began marching forward up the carpeted aisle through the audience. Miss Stacey, smiling warmly in welcome and encouragement, stepped aside so that Gus could step up to the podium.

Facing all the assembled guests, Gus sucked in an enormous breath. He looked as though he were calling upon every scrap of courage he had. His gaze searched the crowd until he found the one face he wanted.

"I, uh...come 'cause...I want to say somethin' to my teacher...Miss King."

Once again, all heads swiveled and all eyes turned to Hetty, whose face was now as pale as Gus's. She was looking at the fiddle and remembering her grim words to the boy about it. What kind of madness, she wondered, was Gus up to now?

Gus gulped in another lungful of air. Never taking his eyes from Hetty, he addressed her directly, as though she were the only person in the room.

"You was the first one who ever tried to help me in my life, Miss King. Ya got me to go to school. Ya learned me how to chew ten times, so I won't burp. If it wasn't for you, I wouldn't know nothin' 'bout learning and about gettin' an education."

After this immense oration, Gus's tongue seemed to give out on him. So, as though turning to a language he knew far better than words, Gus lifted up his bow to his fiddle and began to play.

From the first note, magic permeated the ballroom. This music was none of the hectic reels and jigs he stomped out for the cannery workers. It was slow, like a waltz, and sweet as the first birdsong of spring. The fiddle spoke for Gus in a voice that soared and swayed and sang, and it would have been a hard heart indeed that was not touched by the lad's simple offering. The whole audience sat transfixed, barely breathing, through the tribute. Olivia's lips quivered, and even the Lieutenant Governor's breast heaved suspiciously under its gleaming row of medals.

As for Hetty King, she moved not a hair, and she didn't see the faces of the people around her, the familiar, everyday people of Avonlea who, all as one, forgot Hetty's foibles and thanked her silently, too. Hetty's eyes were fixed on Gus. A great lump swelled in her throat. Tears glittered under her lashes, hinting at a deep well of emotion rarely suspected in the prickly schoolmistress. Those tears might have spilled down altogether had not Gus's music sighed to an end and the Lieutenant Governor leaped to his feet, clapping and cheering.

"Bravo, bravo," the Lieutenant Governor cried.

"Bravo!" the crowd echoed, also rising up as one in a standing ovation. All the schoolchildren, standing to the side and clutching large cardboard lobsters for their musical number, clapped madly too, even Felix. Hetty smiled up at Gus, so proud she was in danger of bursting her corset laces. Seeing Hetty's look, Gus nodded and smiled back, knowing his tribute was truly taken in and understood. Miss Stacey dabbed at her eyes with her handkerchief, openly recognizing that no ditty the class could muster would ever measure up to this.

When Gus slipped his fiddle under his arm and stepped down, he did so with a new confidence in himself and a new trust in the future. Though a mere cannery boy might have been out of place among all those finely dressed personages, there was an air about Gus that declared he had as much right as even the Lieutenant Governor to stand before the crowd. Gus Pike had proved himself a gentleman, in the very finest sense of the word.

❧   ❧   ❧

Skylark takes you on the...

Road to Avonlea*

**Based on the Sullivan Films production adapted from the novels of
LUCY MAUD MONTGOMERY**

☐ **THE JOURNEY BEGINS**, Book #1 $3.99/NCR   48027-8

☐ **THE STORY GIRL EARNS HER NAME**, Book #2 $3.99/NCR   48028-6

☐ **SONG OF THE NIGHT**, Book #3 $3.99/NCR   48029-4

☐ **THE MATERIALIZING OF DUNCAN** $3.99/NCR   48030-8
    MCTAVISH, Book #4

☐ **QUARANTINE AT ALEXANDER** $3.99/NCR   48031-6
    ABRAHAM'S, Book #5

☐ **CONVERSIONS**, Book #6 $3.99/NCR   48032-4

☐ **AUNT ABIGAIL'S BEAU**, Book #7 $3.99/NCR   48033-2

☐ **MALCOLM AND THE BABY**, Book #8 $3.99/NCR   48034-0

☐ **FELICITY'S CHALLENGE**, Book #9 $3.99/NCR   48035-9

☐ **THE HOPE CHEST OF ARABELLA KING**, Book #10 $3.99/NCR   48036-7

☐ **NOTHING ENDURES BUT CHANGE**, Book #11 $3.99/NCR   48037-5

☐ **SARA'S HOMECOMING**, Book #12 $3.99/NCR   48038-3

*ROAD TO AVONLEA is the trademark of Sullivan Films Inc.

By L. M. Montgomery,
the author of

Come to Prince Edward Island
for fun and adventure!

Get ready for friendship and romance on magical Prince Edward Island! You'll meet Sara Stanley, the Story Girl, who knows "How Kissing Was Discovered" and the "Tale of the Family Ghost." There's lively Pat Gardiner of Silver Bush and her friend, the mysterious Judy Plum. Jane of Lanternhill dreams of being reunited with her family. And Valancy finds romance in her dreams of The Blue Castle.